Wilhelm Hünermann

# A
# CRUCIFIED
# HEART
## A Novel of St. Herman Joseph

**English Edition: Hubert S. Szanto**

**St. Michael's Abbey**
**Silverado, CA**
**2004**

English edition
2004

*Published by*
St. Michael's Abbey
19292 El Toro Road
Silverado, CA  92676

*Printed by*
Image Realm
6627 McKinley Avenue
Los Angeles, CA  90001


Based on the German edition published in 1953 under the title
*Hermann Josef: Der Mönch von Steinfeld*
by Fränkische Gesellschaftsdruckerei
in Würzburg, Germany

Text translated and printed with the permission
of the Wilhelm Hünermann heirs


Library of Congress Control Number:  2003099177

ISBN  0-9742298-1-4

# Table of Contents

# Preface to the English Translation

It all started in August, 1943. After graduating from the St. Norbert *Gymnasium*[1] in Szombathely, Hungary, I entered the novitiate of St. Michael's Norbertine[2] Abbey in Csorna. During the retreat, before receiving the habit, Wilhelm Hünermann's novel of the life of St. Herman Joseph was read during the meals (it had been newly translated into Hungarian by Dr. Herman Sallér).[3] It was the novicemaster at the time, Father Ladislas Parker, who initiated the reading of the book at table. He later became the founding abbot of St. Michael's Abbey in the new world.

The story of Herman Joseph remained with me. Not in a vivid, obtrusive way, but like a shadow: accompanying me, keeping me in line, helping me to remain faithful to my vocation. I reread the book and got new strength from it again and again.

After ordination my superiors sent me to continue my studies in Innsbruck, Austria, where I encountered the German edition of the book. When I came to the USA in 1954, I began to teach Latin and German to the novices at Our Lady of Daylesford Priory (now Abbey), Pennsylvania (on the Main Line between Philadelphia and Paoli). In his second year of German, one of the novices, Raymond Frank McQuilkin, opted to translate the first part of the novel (chapters one through twelve). He did a very good job, and the translation into English began.

With the suppression of the abbey of Csorna by the Communist regime in Hungary, eight priests managed to escape and found a new Norbertine community in Santa Ana, California. The priests taught at Mater Dei High School[4] beginning in the fall of 1957. These pioneering Norbertines (among whose number I found myself) went on to open a monastery and Junior Seminary which eventually grew into St. Michael's Abbey and St. Michael's Prep School (located in Silverado, California in the diocese of Orange). When we started the Junior Seminary, the remembrance of St. Herman Joseph was fostered among the students in a subtle way. This continued among the students of the Prep School. The members of the Advanced German class of St. Michael's Prep in the 1976/77 school year (Peter Berghammer, David DeClue, Albert Gurries and Randy Severance) translated the second part of the book (chapters thirteen through twenty-five). They were all members of the Class of 1977. Father Hermann Joseph Rettig, a seminarian at the time, corrected and arranged the text. He also translated the poetry.

McQuilkin's translation (the first part of the novel) was replicated by the thermofax process by Mr. Leer, a pharmacist in Costa Mesa. Mrs. Regina Smith, mother of Fathers James & Philip Smith, typed the entire translation of the book on stencils and we printed several copies on our mimeograph machine.

Meanwhile, Father Hermann Joseph Rettig went to Rome to study theology. In May, 1984, he presented his Master of Arts thesis at the *Angelicum* entitled "*Summi Regis Cor Aveto*: The First Hymn to the Sacred Heart," proving from many sources that this was, indeed, the first ever hymn written to the Sacred Heart. He dedicated his study to me.

In the same year, the Hungarian translation of the historical novel of Hünermann was reprinted through the assistance of the "*Pastorale Ungarnhilfe*" in Vienna, Austria. St. Michael's Abbey of The Norbertine Fathers of Orange financed the venture. The "*Pastorale Ungarnhilfe*" was somewhat reluctant to print the book and wanted to use the money for something else. I, however, was very firm that it had to be the Herman Joseph book.

In the spring of 1994 Mohammad Al-Hamad and other students of St. Michael's Prep input both parts of the book on a computer disk at the initiative of Rev. Gabriel Stack. This disk was given to Richard Martinez, class of 1978, who rewrote the entire book and put it into attractive, contemporary English. In October, 1997, Richard finished the first draft of rewriting. Mrs. Betty Vaughan read through the whole text and made the necessary grammatical and spelling corrections. Mrs. Teri Firmin generously donated $10,000.00 toward the printing cost. The photos of the artwork in the book are courtesy of James & Rosario Gonzalez, Richard Belcher and Rev. Joseph Horn. The cover design was the joint project of Rev. Godfrey Bushmaker and Rev. Norbert Wood. The final editing of the book was done by Rev. Norbert Wood who also added the historical afterword, chronology and bibliography. He was assisted by frater Ambrose Criste.

Although Herman Joseph was recognized as "Blessed" by Pope Benedict XIII on January 22, 1728, it was not until August 11, 1958, that Pope Pius XII declared him a Saint.[5] The movers behind this declaration were the archbishop of Cologne and the bishop of

Aachen.  The Norbertine Order for the most part was just a silent bystander.  Somehow I cannot escape the notion that the Norbertine Order was always busy working and doing things and did not care much for publicity throughout its long history.  The canonization of its founder, St. Norbert,[6] and the erection of his statue in St. Peter's in Rome,[7] come to mind in this vein!

The date of the feast of St. Herman Joseph was shifted during the liturgical reorganization after Vatican II to May 24.  At St. Michael's Abbey he is celebrated as the patron of youth and the day holds the rank of a feast.


St. Michael's Abbey has several original works of art depicting St. Herman Joseph.  I contacted Wolfgang Köberl, a well-known Austrian painter living in Innsbruck, and asked him to paint two pictures of Herman Joseph: one in the traditional setting of presenting the apple to the Child Jesus and the other in the rather neglected scene of writing the first ever hymn to the Sacred Heart.  These two paintings currently hang above the altar in the Cardinal Mindszenty Chapel.

Bill Conger of Garden Grove, an amateur artist, created three statues which he donated to the monastery in the early sixties: St. Michael, which was destroyed by vandals who wanted his shield; Our Lady of Guadalupe, which is on the side of the hill near the current sisters' convent; and the group setting in the "cactus garden," which depicts the Crucified Christ appearing to Herman Joseph while writing his hymn to the Sacred Heart (we also have from Mr. Conger a wood-carved heart within a flame with a small figure of the Crucified Christ in the heart.)

In the abbey church at St. Michael's there is a window honoring St. Herman Joseph.  It was donated by the class of 1986.  A second window in the working sacristy is also dedicated to Herman Joseph.  It depicts Herman Joseph drawing water from a pure mountain stream above his abbey of Steinfeld for use at the Holy Sacrifice of the Mass.  Both windows were created by John Bera Studios of San Diego.

Fr. Vincent Gilmore created a beautiful shrine in the student dormitory for a European woodcarving of the little Herman Joseph offering an apple to the Child Jesus held by the Blessed Mother.

It is a reminder to the students that Herman Joseph is the patron of youth educated in Norbertine Schools.

In April, 1997, the alumni honored me by presenting the abbey with a statue of St. Herman Joseph modeled after an ancient statue in the abbey of Steinfeld,[8] Germany (where Herman Joseph lived in the twelfth and thirteenth centuries). The statue is now located in the sacristy. In addition to the various works of art honoring St. Herman Joseph, Father James Smith brought us a relic given to him by the Salvatorian provincial at Steinfeld.

The various depictions of St. Herman Joseph at St. Michael's Abbey referred to above are all reproduced in the photographs in this book (cf. pages 80 - 95).

I offer my heartfelt gratitude to all who have made the present edition possible: as you can see, it was quite a collaborative effort. God bless each and every one of you for your contribution to this worthwhile project!

Rev. Hubert S. Szanto, O.Praem., Ph.D.

7

# Footnotes to the Preface

1    Roughly the equivalent of grades 5 through 12 in the USA. The school was run by the Norbertine Fathers and is also the school where Cardinal Josef Mindszenty received his education.

2    The religious Order founded by St. Norbert of Xanten in 1120 (also known as the "Premonstratensians" or "Canons Regular of Prémontré" after the valley of Prémontré, France,where the first abbey was established). The Order's spirituality is rooted in St. Augustine's vision of the monastic life for priests as interpreted by St. Norbert, a Gregorian reformer of the twelfth century and later archbishop of Magdeburg.

3    Under the title "A Rajna-parti Dóm."

4    The largest Catholic high school west of the Mississippi, founded in 1950 and located in Santa Ana, California.

5    A later document of the Sacred Congregation for Rites on January 15, 1960, under Pope John XXIII, simply responded to certain questions of the Bishop of Aachen regarding the initial decree of 1958. For this reason it is sometimes mistakenly asserted that Herman Joseph was canonized by John XXIII.

6    St. Norbert, who died on June 6, 1134, was not canonized until July 28, 1582. The Order has never had a strong reputation for "pushing" the causes of its many saints.

7    Another long-delayed effort.

8    The abbey eventually became a boys' school run by the Salvatorian Fathers. St. Herman Joseph is buried in the former abbey church and his grave is still the site of pilgrimages and devotion.

# About the Author

Wilhelm Hünermann was born into a family of nine children on July 28, 1900. His birthplace at Kempen on the Lower Rhine, Germany, is well known for also being the birthplace of Thomas a Kempis, the author of *The Imitation of Christ*. In the summer of 1918, just before the end of World War I, Wilhelm was called to military service in the army but the war ended before he could see any combat. In the winter semester of 1918 he entered the seminary and began his studies for the priesthood in Münster. He also felt drawn to study German literature and was a theater director in the seminary. He wrote delightful poems as well as various other pieces and rehearsed classical theater pieces with his study companions. With a dispensation from the pope, he was ordained a priest in Münster at age 22 on May 27, 1923, the feast of St. Bede the Venerable. He was first assigned to Sterckrade in the Ruhr region and shortly after this to Berlin. His parish of St. Matthias was staffed by priests from the diocese of Münster and his pastor was the famous Clement Graf von Galen, the later bishop of Münster, who through his fearless preaching provoked the wrath of the Nazis. At this time Wilhelm was very much involved in the youth apostolate and also wrote for various Catholic publications in Berlin. His next assignment was in Dülken before being named teacher of religion at Düren where he was disciplined by the school for offering a public prayer for the soul of Klausner, the leader of Catholic Action in Berlin, who was murdered by the Nazis. During his years at Düren he had audited classes in German literature at Cologne. After he had to leave Düren, he was named associate pastor at Rheydt in 1935. It was here that he determined to write his first major book entitled "The Baker's Boy of Znaim." The book enjoyed a great success and Fr. Hünermann proceeded immediately with the publication of other books. At the beginning of World War II, in 1939, the Nazis forbade him to publish further. He spent the war in Reydt, where he was bombed out several times and lost numerous books from his extensive personal library. Immediately after the War he took up his literary activity again (he had prepared a number of manuscripts during the War). All of his literary activity had to be accomplished in his free time alongside his demanding duties in the care of souls. In the years after the War he was responsible for the diocesan newspaper of Aachen for about two years. Thereafter he was freed by the bishop of Aachen to pursue his literary work full time and lived since the fifties at Essen in the Ruhr region. He died shortly after celebrating the golden jubilee of his ordination to the priesthood. Wilhelm Hünermann was one of the most significant and widely read religious novelists of the German speaking world in the twentieth century. Numerous books of his were translated into a total of seventeen different languages. And even today some of his works continue to appear in new editions.

Father Wilhelm Hünermann

# Chapter One
# The Bishop Who Could Not Bless

**A**rnold von Randerode, archbishop of Cologne, awoke with a scream. Blood pounded against his temples, and his brow was wet with sweat. He tried to erase images from the terrible nightmare that had tormented him, but the surrounding darkness of his large bedroom overwhelmed the weak glimmer of light cast by a small oil lamp.

Something was emerging from the palpitating darkness. Something threatening, hostile, and ominous was approaching from all sides to smother him in his bed. The archbishop screamed again as he rang his silver bell, its sound echoing through the night like a cry for help.

Then he listened, not daring to breathe – and *listened*. *Nothing!* Yet he sensed a giant's hand grasping the columns and arches and vaults of his residence. The sound of his bell rang out again and again in the darkness like a cry of despair.

Finally, the door opened. A servant entered, clad in a nightshirt, his wild, white hair illuminated by his flickering candle.

"Your Grace!" the old man wheezed.

"You're finally here!" groaned the bishop. "Come closer. Don't just stand there. Make some more light. Light all the candles! This darkness and gloom are killing me!"

The servant climbed onto a chair with difficulty and began lighting the chandelier's two dozen candles. It took a long time for him to complete his task, and the archbishop said nothing until the old man had finished.

"The light is good. Now I shall be all right."

"You are sick with fever, Your Grace. Shall I call a doctor?"

"No doctor can help me now. My sickness is inside my heart, and no medicine or balm can heal it. But come here, Barthel. Sit with me here. I want to talk to you."

"But Your Grace!"

"Don't be so formal. Forget for a few moments that I am the bishop. Just think of me as another man."

"Your Grace!?" Barthel exclaimed in wonder.

"It's all right, Barthel. Here, give me your hand. Tell me, how long have you been in my service?"

"More than thirty years, Your Grace. You were still provost at Saint Andrew's when I started. What good days those were...."

"You're right, Barthel. Those were the best of times. Then Bishop Hugo died, and ambition crept into my heart. My family gave me no peace. I was their means to greater power. They tried to press gold into my hands, and I resisted as long as I could. But finally I opened the cathedral door with a *golden key*. Did you hear what I said, Barthel?!"

"You should sleep, my Lord," stammered the servant.

"I cannot sleep. I must tell you. It tortures me to conceal it. As I said, with a *golden key* I opened the cathedral door. Do you know what that is called, Barthel?"

"Your Grace, I beseech you, do not force me to answer."

"Barthel! I want you to say the word to my face!"

"The Church calls it... *simony*. Howev..."

"However nothing! You are right, Barthel. It's called simony! But there was a monk, a saint the people say, Bernard, the abbot of Clairvaux. He petitioned Pope Eugene, and I was called before his council. In my stubbornness I refused to attend. Pope Eugene then suspended me from exercising my episcopal functions. I was unable to consecrate and bless and my hands became powerless. I have enjoyed no peace since that day, Barthel, only fears, horrors, and afflictions. Please get me a glass of water. My lips are burning. It is a fever whose source is deep within me."

The archbishop emptied the glass in two gulps, then heaved a sigh and continued. "God has sent His plagues to this city bereft of a bishop's blessing. And when the people rioted against me, I clenched these hands which could not bless into fists, and struck down my own children. And God sent scourge after scourge. What happened to Cologne in the year 1148, Barthel?"

"The plague."

"And in '49?"

"Half the city went up in flames."

"And in '50?"

"Crop failure and famine."

"And the people of Cologne, to whom do they attribute these disasters?"

"I do not know, Your Grace. I am seldom among the people."

"You *do* know, Barthel. Tell me!" gasped the feverish bishop as he shook the old man's shoulders. "By God, tell the truth!"

12

"The people, uh, they say that, uh, all our misfortune..."

"Continue!" bellowed the archbishop.

"...came from the fact that the city, uh, has a bishop... who cannot bless!" The old man tried to swallow his words, and the bishop recoiled against his pillow and groaned.

"It's not over, Barthel. Our time of scourges has not passed. I have seen it in a dream, rushing from the mountains, swallowing the valleys – a monster against which Cologne is defenseless. A flood! Do you hear? Already it is beginning to rumble!"

"The Rhine is rising, Your Grace, but Cologne's dams are good."

"Where is there a dam strong enough to withstand God's fury?!"

Just then the blaring of the flood guard's horn sent both men running to the window for a view of the city below. Screams filled the night as the dam was indeed succumbing to the Rhine's overwhelming force. Water had broken through and was filling the streets of the city.

After instructing Barthel to leave the palace with the rest of his staff, Archbishop Arnold von Randerode sat alone at his bedroom window, in anguish on account of his city's suffering. The bells rang out from churches throughout Cologne, blending with the shrill cries of terror to produce a cacophony of despair.

The archbishop raised his right hand as if to make the sign of the Cross over this scene of horror. Then he let it drop as he cried out to his city, "Cologne! Here stands your bishop. He has no blessing for you!"

Then he collapsed to the floor.

\* \* \*

That same hour, a cloth merchant named Christopher raced down a dark staircase to his storage cellar on Stephan Street. Water had burst through his cellar window and was rising up the stairs. He could not open the cellar door, so he risked entering through the broken window to save his giant rolls of fine Flemish velvet, silk, and brocade. He left his lantern halfway up the stairs before wading into the water.

The ice cold water seemed to knock the air from his lungs, and red spots danced before his eyes, but he threw himself into the water in a futile attempt to save some small remnant of his stock. He was unable to drag the waterlogged rolls of cloth out the cellar window. Christopher fell into the freezing cold water several times in his effort to avoid the inevitable.

"Lost! All lost! Oh, God, Your Hand is heavy!"

Then he heard a baby's cry and struggled out the cellar window and up the stairs to his living quarters where his wife Maria had been ready to give birth to their first child. Christopher wondered how so much could happen in one night. "Dear God, please protect my wife and new child!"

Christopher entered the room where his wife Maria was. Katherine, the midwife, gazed upon the dripping wet figure and said, "You have a son!"

Christopher felt neither the chill nor the fever racing through him. He did not feel how soaking wet he was. He saw only his newborn son. Then he knelt at his wife's bedside and, overcome with emotion, he began to cry. His wife stroked his wet hair with her pale hand.

"All the cloth is ruined, Maria," he said. "All is lost!"

"No, Christopher," his wife whispered almost inaudibly. "God has blessed us. We have a child."

\* \* \*

Archbishop Arnold awoke from unconsciousness hours later. He saw at his bedside a monk in a white tunic whose hands were folded beneath his black scapular. An almost fiery gleam blazed forth from his eyes as he stared down at the bishop. Arnold recognized him immediately.

"Abbot Bernard of Clairvaux!"

"Arnold von Randerode! Cologne has suffered many sorrows because of you. Lay down the crosier which you obtained with gold. How will you stand before the judgment seat of God?"

The bishop groaned before he responded in a voice that reflected his weakness and sorrow. "I need not lay down my crosier, Abbot Bernard. Someone is fast approaching who will seize it from me – *death!* Come nearer, Lord Abbot, and give me your hand. I bore enmity toward you, but now I know that you were right.

Forgive me. Will you not share a comforting word to give me strength? I am terrified of my eternal judgment!"

"God does not wish the death of the sinner, but that he be converted and live." The strength of the abbot's voice was softened by its rich and comforting resonance.

"There is much comfort in the truth. Thank you, Abbot Bernard." Then, gripping the monk's hand as tightly as he could, the archbishop pleaded once more, "There is still another fear which torments me. I fear for Cologne. God continues to vent His wrath upon this city. Have you no words which can console me?"

The monk uttered his prophetic response: "On account of your sins, Arnold von Randerode, God has smitten this city. On account of your repentance, He will bless it." The abbot walked to the window, opened the shutters, and looked out over the beleaguered city. "God blesses you, Cologne! Where the arches of your burnt cathedral stare into darkness, there a new sanctuary will rise. Its towers will soar high toward the light like arms reaching up to heaven. God will bless you, Cologne! And I see something else, something much greater than the cathedral which will rise one day. God blesses you even more abundantly, Cologne, for He sends you a grace which contains the riches of heaven. This night, Cologne, God sends you a child on whose head His blessing rests. In this night of misery, Cologne, in you a saint is born!"

＊ ＊ ＊

Two weeks after the great flood, Maria returned to the Capitol church for the first time. She carried her newborn child, who had been baptized with the name of "Herman." Maria knelt before the statue of the Little Madonna and lifted her son to the Heavenly Mother: "I bring you my child, Mother. Protect him as you protected your own Child. Preserve him in grace, O clement, O loving, O sweet Virgin Mary!"

The Little Madonna certainly had her hands full as of late, aiding and comforting the people of Cologne whose misfortunes drove them to her feet. The floodwaters had receded and the dam was being repaired and fortified, but much misery still remained.

Many images of the Madonna adorned the holy city of Cologne, most of them depicting Mary in regal splendor. The statue of the Little Madonna of the Capitol church was different, however. Here Mary was not seated, but she stood and looked at her children so kindly, as if to say, "Come to me! Tell me what burdens your heart. I am your Mother. You can always come to me."

Maria was walking home from her visit to the church when she heard the somber tolling of its bells. Word soon spread throughout the streets that the archbishop had died. Maria prayed for God's mercy upon his soul as she pressed her child more closely to her breast.


Three days later, the archbishop was buried in the church of Saint Andrew.

# Chapter Two
# The Cook of Sankt Mergen

**S**ister Iburga stood before the kitchen fire stirring a huge pot of soup with a large wooden spoon. She was the cook of "Sankt Mergen," as the Capitol church was called in old Cologne. She enjoyed her work immensely. Her face was glowing with steam which warmed and soothed her. She let go of the spoon, allowing it to swirl in the boiling soup as she closed her eyes. Just then she felt a tug on her apron.

"What do you want!?" Iburga snapped at Gertrude, the young kitchen helper.

"The venerable Sister Prioress has asked me to remind you that tomorrow is the feast of our Blessed Mother's Annunciation."

"I know that!" growled Sister Iburga as she tried to reclaim her swirling spoon.

"And since it is a great feast, Sister Prioress said you would honor our Blessed Mother by preparing something special for the convent table."

"Sister Prioress is a glutton!" hissed the cook, whose apron grew more stained and soiled with each successive stir.

"The venerable Sister Prioress mentioned that she saw some fat hens that would bake most excellently. She said she saw them at…"

"Sister Prioress is a fat hen herself! Besides, I rule the kitchen and the cellar, not the prioress!" As she spoke, she wielded her spoon as though it were a scepter. Iburga was the descendent of thirty-two noble ancestors, twice the number required for entrance into the convent of Sankt Mergen. Her father was a count who ruled a castle and one hundred soldiers in the Lower Rhineland. "Besides, a more suitable honor for Our Lady would be to thicken the soup for the poor with those chickens. Now then, Gertrude, help me carry this pot to the gate. God's poor people are waiting hungry while we discuss feasting."

Sister Iburga enforced strict order among her "guests" at the convent door. In the six years since the great flood, the crowds increased so dramatically that the cook's stern nature was needed to maintain order. However, she also shared a comforting and encouraging word with each one who passed through her line.

A six-year-old boy raised his bowl to Sister Iburga, who could never resist his imploring smile and penetrating blue eyes. She dipped into the pot for some good pieces of meat to add to his soup. "May God reward you, Sister Iburga!" chirped the small boy with the bright voice. "Mother says that in heaven you will get a golden throne with a velvet pillow for your goodness."

"Did your mother really say that?" laughed the cook.

"Truly she did. I'm not lying!" the boy insisted. "I think she also said that you would get a *red* velvet pillow!"

"So, a *red* one! But tell me, Herman, how is your father?"

"Oh, he still coughs so much," he said sadly.

"Then you must pray much," Iburga urged.

"I pray to Mother Mary all day long!" Herman responded eagerly. "But now I must go home before the soup gets cold."

"Wait a minute, Herman," the cook said. Her hands fumbled in her pockets before she presented him with a beautiful red apple. "Here. This is for the red velvet pillow."

"Oh thank you, Sister Iburga! An apple this wonderful *must* be from the convent garden, from the last tree way in the corner."

"Look how much you know about our garden. But go now, Herman. Many more people want soup, and we mustn't keep them waiting."

Since the Capitol church was right next door, Herman decided to stop in for a moment to pray. The soup could wait for that. He had to push one of the doors of Sankt Mergen open with his foot. Today he had no time to admire the beautiful and intricate carvings which adorned it. The heavy pot of soup also prevented him from dipping his hand into the holy water.

Herman struggled to reach the statue of the Little Madonna which was his favorite, and he heaved a heavy sigh after releasing his grip from the steaming pot. Then he knelt on the steps of the Blessed Mother's altar, folded his hands, and prayed the glorious prayer which the crusader-preacher Bernard had taught the people of Cologne. Now it echoed throughout the churches and within the hearts of Cologne: "*Salve, Regina!*" "Hail, Holy Queen!" Then Herman spoke to his Holy Mother with his own simple, innocent, and loving words.

* * *

Sister Iburga's red velvet-cushioned, heavenly, golden throne was soon transformed into the uncomfortable, wooden chair directly across from her glaring superior. The ingenuous Gertrude had repeated to the prioress all that Iburga had said about her. Sister Prioress then told the abbess, Mother Adelaide, whose stern demeanor told Iburga that she had not been summoned for a commendation.

"You have seriously offended the law of charity, and what makes it worse is that you have scandalized our kitchen girl. You could have damaged her esteem for Sister Prioress. Is that the proper example to set for Gertrude?" the abbess asked.

"I know I said she was a glutton, but it was not intended in such a mean spirit. And the 'fat hen' came out unexpectedly. Now I understand that it resulted from not holding my tongue in the first place."

The abbess nodded. "You must apologize to Sister Prioress. Now go to the church and ask our Blessed Mother to give you a bit more patience and gentleness."

"I will gladly do that. And then I will proceed to the store where I can buy Sister Prioress her chickens."

"That isn't necessary, Iburga," smiled Mother Adelaide. "You are right to say that improving the poor people's soup honors the Mother of God. Do so, and Sister Prioress will also be content if she thinks it over."

The cook of Sankt Mergen passed through the church door to do her penance before the statue of the Virgin Mary. She was surprised to notice little Herman kneeling in prayer before Mary's altar. She had sent him off nearly an hour ago. With pride she remembered the good meat she had saved for the boy, who failed to notice her approach. His eyes were transfixed on the statue of the Madonna, but his hands, which had been so peacefully folded, were now extended in supplication.

"Please, Mother Mary, ask your Son to heal my father. Maybe you could whisper my request into His ear. Then father will not cough any more, and mother will not cry so much, and Sister Iburga won't have to cook any more soup for us. If we were not so poor, Mother Mary, I would give you something for hearing my prayer." The boy looked at the pot beside him. "Surely you have better soup in heaven."

Sister Iburga winced before realizing that it was her pride that caused her to be here in the first place. She felt that something miraculous was about to happen. "Wait a minute." The boy fumbled through the pockets of his pants. "Here! Look at this apple. Sister Iburga gave it to me. It is a heavenly apple, so truly you deserve it. Here, Mother! Take my apple!"

Sister Iburga knelt spellbound, her heart pounding fiercely as she watched the miraculous scene unfold before her eyes. The boy climbed toward the statue of the Little Madonna. Then he reached up to her and held out his apple.

"Take it, Mother. Please put out your hand!"

A brilliant, golden radiance enveloped the altar and the child. Sister Iburga was momentarily blinded, but she cried out when she could see again. The statue of the Little Madonna was no longer there. Mary, the Queen of Heaven herself, stood there instead, holding the Divine Child in her arms. Herman continued to extend the apple toward his Heavenly Mother.

Then Sister Iburga witnessed a miracle of love as Mary smiled and extended her hand. The boy laid the apple in it, and, once again, she smiled. Overwhelmed, Sister Iburga covered her face. Then she heard Herman's voice again:

"Don't forget my father, Mother Mary!"

Sister looked up again to see the statue of the Little Madonna over the altar. Herman quietly came down the stairs, picked up his pot of soup, and left the church with a wobbly gait.

Sister Iburga recounted the experience to the abbess, at times doubting what she had seen. Mother Adelaide said she had been immeasurably blessed to witness such a miracle. "Miracles are not so strange on earth. And why shouldn't our Blessed Lady perform a miracle for a child whose love impels him closer to her and her Son? You have witnessed a miracle, Iburga. You saw our Heavenly Mother hear the prayers of a child whose heart is pure."

The next day Sister Iburga, her face beaming, surprised Sister Prioress. "Forgive me, Sister, for the mean names I called you. But I thank you a thousand times for telling Mother Abbess. Because you did, I witnessed a miracle!" Smiling, she listened to the hundreds of bells which joyously proclaimed throughout Cologne the feast of the Annunciation.

# Chapter Three
# Saint Joseph's Pretzels

**M**artin the shoemaker and his five-year-old daughter Margaret were visiting friends after attending Mass on the feast of the Annunciation. He and his sick friend Christopher sat together in the afternoon sunshine soaking in the sun's healing rays.

"I feel much better than yesterday," remarked the former cloth merchant. "The sun is good for my chest."

"You didn't cough at all last night," Frau Maria said as she brought the men some water.

"When the sun shines on my wooden leg, it feels much better, too," added Martin.

"If you can't feel your wooden leg, how does it *feel* better?" asked the inquisitive Herman.

"Don't ask me how," laughed Martin. "I'm a shoemaker, not a doctor!"

"At least you still have your trade," interjected Christopher. "If only I was well again. I could work and we wouldn't have to depend on the Sisters' charity. I'm ashamed of how much we rely on them."

"Poverty certainly hurts," added Martin. "I am working, and yet still we have so little. If I had any extra, I would surely share it with you."

"Father, is poverty bad?" Herman asked quickly before Christopher could thank his friend for the kind thought.

"Very bad," his father answered.

"Are we poor?"

"Very poor."

"Then are *we* bad?" Herman asked, approaching his father.

"*We* are not, but poverty is," Christopher explained.

"Weren't Jesus, Mary, and Joseph also very poor?"

"Of course."

"Then poverty is not bad!" decided Herman enthusiastically, and returned to playing with Margaret and the fluffy white cat she had brought.

"The boy speaks wisdom beyond his years!" remarked the shoemaker.

"Herman knows everything!" proclaimed his daughter as she looked respectfully at the boy who was a whole year and half older and a full head taller than she.

Herman, however, grew uncomfortable with such extravagant praise. "Tell us a story about the Crusades, Master Martin!" he cried, knowing that the expert storyteller didn't need much prodding.

"Well, gather 'round then, and I will tell you a story. The crusaders traveled from Cologne in the year 1147. Abbot Bernard of Clairvaux, he is a saint you know, had so inflamed my heart with his preaching that I put away my tools, took off my apron, kissed my wife goodbye, and told her that she'd see me return as a hero or never see me again. 'The poor Sultan!' she sighed, shedding a few tears. To this day, I don't know whether they were shed for me or the Sultan." Then the shoemaker paused dramatically.

"Continue the story!" clamored the children, who had propped themselves up on the knees of the former crusader.

"Ah, yes.... And so, we left. More than two hundred ships filled with crusaders from Flanders and England joined us. We traveled south until we anchored in Lisbon where there were two-hundred-and-fifty thousand Saracen soldiers and even more heathens.

"We soon captured the land surrounding the city, but Lisbon itself is built upon high rocks and is further protected by massive walls. All our attacks could not force a surrender. We besieged the city for four long months. Food ran short. There was only enough for the soldiers, so the people resorted to eating dogs, cats, and even vermin.

"We stormed the city for the last time on October twenty-first. We wanted to win the city, but we wanted even more to travel on to our intended destination: the Holy Land! The Spanish riders attacked first, but the Saracens behind the walls only laughed at their feeble attempt. When those infidels heard the battle cry of the men from Cologne, though, their hearts fell into their silk breeches. They threw down their weapons and begged for mercy before we even assaulted the walls. Then the city doors flew open, and we raised the standard of Christ from every tower in Lisbon!"

Herman's eyes were aglow as he listened, but they grew a bit cloudy with doubt at the end. "They just threw down their weapons when they saw you?"

"It's the truth! Remember the date, young Herman: the twenty-first of October."

"The Feast of Saint Ursula and the eleven-thousand Virgins!"

"Correct. And many crusaders said they saw the eleven-thousand appear in golden armor! That's when the Mohammedans succumbed to their fear. Saint Ursula and the eleven-thousand Virgins never desert a citizen of Cologne. Remember Attila, the leader of the Huns? When he and his men tried to besiege Cologne, the eleven-thousand Virgins appeared and drove them to flight."

"That's true!" Herman eagerly confirmed. "Sisters from the convent of Saint Ursula have told me that many times. But what happened to the Crusade, Master Martin?"

"Well, then we traveled to the Holy Land...."

"And?"

"And they cut off my leg, the infidel mongrels!"

"Did you conquer Jerusalem?"

"Well... we... eh..." Martin scratched his head as his eyes searched the sky for some suitable response. There was none, however, for in fact the Crusade did not end gloriously. "That I will tell you another time."

"When will the next Crusade leave?" Herman asked.

"I don't know if there will be another one, Herman, but perhaps our new ruler, Emperor Frederick of Swabia, will risk it. He is said to be a powerful leader."

"I will follow our emperor to the Holy Land!" shouted Herman.

"I will go too!" Margaret cried with conviction.

"No," retorted Herman. "You must stay here and wipe your tears with your apron!"

Martin exploded with laughter while the boy's father and mother exchanged a knowing glance. Then Margaret realized that her cat had disappeared, and she began to cry. The story of the Crusade had been too captivating for her to notice its escape.

"Can we go look for it, Mother?" Herman pleaded.

"Yes, go!"

"You have a strange child, Christopher," Martin said as the children disappeared out the door. "The boy asks questions that are well beyond his years; and his eyes, that child has such eyes."

Frau Maria listened silently. Since her son's birth she knew that God had blessed her and her husband in a singular manner.

"The cat has surely run off to Lichhof," said Herman. "There are so many trees there." Margaret agreed, of course, so the two children walked down Stephan Street past the Capitol church to Lichhof, the cemetery of Sankt Mergen.

When the cat could not be found in the graveyard, the two youngsters walked hand in hand back to the Capitol church. There they marveled at the elaborate carvings on the huge, wooden doors. The entire life of Jesus, from the Annunciation to the Ascension, was masterfully carved into the old wood. The details fascinated the children: the dog putting its tail between its legs when the angel appeared to the shepherds; the ox and the ass whose breath warmed the new-born Child in the crib; the evil King Herod; the flight into Egypt. Herman explained each scene and story to Margaret, who was awed by what she both saw and heard.

"*He* has it!" Herman suddenly blurted out.

"*Who* has it?"

"Saint Joseph has it!"

"What does he have?" Margaret asked.

"*Poverty!* Just look at the flight into Egypt. Saint Joseph is pulling the donkey that holds Our Lady and Our Lord. Do you see any basket of food with them, Margaret?"

"No."

"The only thing they have to eat is hanging from Saint Joseph's staff."

"Thick sausages!" observed a delighted Margaret.

"Those aren't sausages. They're pretzels! You know, two pretzels, like the ones Sister Iburga hands out on fast days. That must be it. Saint Joseph passed Sankt Mergen on his flight into Egypt, and the Sister cook gave him two pretzels."

"You do know everything, Herman!" Margaret said.

"Saint Joseph must really have been poor if he got pretzels from Sankt Mergen. And Saint Joseph wasn't evil, he was holy! That's why poverty is also holy!"

A long period of silence followed as the children continued walking. Then Margaret asked, "Are you certain you will go on the Crusade?"

"Absolutely certain."

"Where is the Holy Land?"

"Very far away. The heathens live there."

"Did the heathens also live in Egypt?"

"Yes."

"But Saint Joseph didn't take a sword with him to kill the heathens. He carried only his staff and two pretzels."

"But he had Mary, and she carried Jesus. The heathens surely were converted when Joseph showed them our Savior and His Mother."

"Then what is better, Herman," Margaret asked, "to kill the heathens or to convert them?"

"Convert them, of course," Herman answered.

"Then you must not be a Crusader, Herman. You must get two pretzels from Sister Iburga and then go and show Mary and Jesus to the heathens. They will surely be converted."

Herman thought a long time about what Margaret had said.

"You're right, Margaret! If I could be like Saint Joseph, I could show Jesus and Mary to the entire world! Of course Sister Iburga would have to give me a few more pretzels.... Listen, Margaret, let's go ask our Blessed Mother herself!"

The children devoutly entered the rear of the church and headed toward the choir loft, under which stood the gated entryway into the nave and altars of the church.

"Oh no! The choir grating is locked!"

The children gripped the iron bars and gazed up at the statue of the Little Madonna which was aglow with light from the votive candles. Herman felt the attraction of his Heavenly Mother and even the urging of the Child in her arms.

"I'm going to climb over!" Herman whispered to Margaret.

"That's too dangerous, Herman. You'll surely fall down!"

"I will surely climb over! The Mother of God is standing right there. What could possibly happen to me?"

Herman gripped the bars and began to climb up the grating. As he swung himself over, a violent pain came upon him. Herman cried out.

"What's the matter?" Margaret shrieked.

"It feels like a nail has pierced my heart! But my body is fine. What a sharp pain!"

Herman then climbed down the gate and proceeded without delay to Mary's altar. Margaret watched with a sense of reverence as the boy spoke openly before his favorite statue. Then she shielded her eyes from a sudden and overwhelming light, to which her eyes quickly adjusted. It seemed to Margaret that Herman was playing games with Our Lady and her Child. She rubbed her eyes repeatedly, and yet the marvel continued. Then it was over.

Herman did not return to the gate for a long time, but Margaret felt no sense of urgency. She was still delighting in the heavenly scene played out before her. She noticed that Herman's eyes shone more brightly than she had ever seen them before. He eventually returned and silently took her hand as they left the church. They stopped to look once more at the carvings on the door, and another piercing pain caused Herman to cringe.

"Margaret, you're right! To be like Saint Joseph is better than to be a crusader."

"Does it still hurt?" Margaret asked.

"Very much, but I don't know what it is."

\* \* \*

At that very same hour, Abbess Hildegard was walking with one of her Sisters through the cloister garden of Rupertsberg-at-Bingen. The Sister had become discouraged by the thorny path which stood between herself and ultimate union with God.

"Dear Sister," the abbess remarked, "most of us, including those of good will, only *approach* the barrier behind which God hides Himself. But those whom God embraces with special love, He pulls over that barrier into His full light. And that heart must respond to God's call by suffering. So go, Sister, and accept your crosses cheerfully, for you are abundantly blessed."

\* \* \*

The two children walked silently through Stephan Street. Before they entered Herman's home, he requested a favor of Margaret.

"From now on, will you please call me 'Joseph'? But no one must hear you; it will be our secret."

"Yes, I will, *Joseph!*"

## Chapter Four

# The Flaming Cross

**H**erman jumped up from his bed in the middle of the night. Once again he was seized by the searing sting which continued to penetrate his heart since that day two years ago when he climbed over the gate in the church of Sankt Mergen. But there was something else.

Herman rubbed his eyes, got out of bed, and opened the window of the attic. Then he let out a scream. The sky before him was a seething ocean of red heat. Flames surged and splashed among the rooftops in the distance. The fireguard blew the horn of warning as the bells from Saint Martin's and Sankt Mergen began to peal. Herman ran downstairs as his father was coming to get him.

"The fire is on Martin Street!" he gasped. "If the wind blows in from the Rhine, the fire will reach us!"

"Christ be with us!" exclaimed Frau Maria. "All you saints, stand by us!"

Herman and his father quickly dressed and ran outside to help. They were immediately overcome by the glare of the fire, which voraciously feasted on the old wooden cottages and houses. People were running the opposite direction, their faces smeared with soot and bleached with terror. A few were carrying possessions. Screaming children clung to their mothers. The father and son heard demented laughter and saw a man dancing with a burning board amidst the rubble of a home. They dodged through the streets as a roof collapsed to their left, a wall succumbed to the flames on the right, and showers of sparks rained down almost everywhere.

They finally ran past Sankt Mergen to Martin Street, where a chain of firefighters had already assembled. Buckets of water flew from hand to hand. The heat was almost unbearable, and men wet their faces with the water that spilled from the buckets. To these brave men of Cologne, disaster was no stranger.

Although only eight years old, Herman entered the line and passed pails of water until his small arms were rendered powerless. He staggered out of the line and sank onto a doorstep. His chest heaved, struggling for breath as the smoke and heat burned in his throat.

Suddenly, he saw a priest walking down the burning street. It was the pastor of Saint Martin's. He had been burned, but he walked with a reverent though unsteady gait. He carried a large ciborium toward Sankt Mergen. Herman immediately knelt down on the cobblestones as the Word-Made-Flesh proceeded through the hellish streets of Cologne.

Then Herman realized that Saint Martin's must be on fire. He stared through the flames to the spot where the church roof should stand. There the flames parted and the belfry stood out amidst the fire and smoke. Herman then saw flames licking at the roof from all sides. He cried out that the church must be saved, but no one heard him in the tremendous noise and confusion. Even if he had been heard, no one would have risked passing through the sea of flames to reach the house of God. The church seemed doomed.

Herman saw the flames ascend, dancing eagerly around the Cross. Then, suddenly and mysteriously, the crucifix grew larger and was elevated up into the red sky. On the Cross, Herman saw the body of Jesus surrounded by the flames. Then Herman saw Jesus spread out His arms over His church, and the flames receded and diminished. In the midst of the raging inferno, Saint Martin's stood untouched.

"It's a miracle!" Herman shouted.

Herman made his way to the hay market to look at the church from the other side. Again he saw the Cross of the Lord high above the flames, and again he saw the outstretched arms of Jesus protecting His holy church. Herman ran past the apple market to the Jewish quarter. There he still saw Jesus standing guard over His dwelling place.

Hot wind buffeted the boy's cheeks, but he continued to stare at the miracle in the midst of the terror. It seemed as if the whole world was succumbing to the flames, and that the church of St. Martin's was like Golgotha on top of which stood the Cross. Wherever the Lord stretched out His tortured arms, the fire was extinguished, its flames driven into His pierced side. The heat of the destruction was transformed into the eternal fire of love contained within the Sacred Heart of Jesus.

The fire raged throughout the night until the wind began to blow back toward the Rhine. Only at the broad streets of the marketplace were the flames finally extinguished. Entire districts of the city lay in burnt destruction. The church of Saint Martin's remained untouched, however. The next morning, the pastor returned the Blessed Sacrament to the sanctuary surrounded by misery and offered the Holy Sacrifice of the Mass for his devastated parish.

* * *

Herman lay in bed for days, losing and then regaining consciousness because of a high fever. After the fire he had been found lying on a doorstep, covered with soot. Since then, his mother had been constantly at his bedside, cooling his brow with a wet cloth. Herman cried out in his feverish dreams, "Put out Your arms! Stretch them out!" Then he would sink again into apparent death.

After a week in this condition, Herman regained full consciousness. His fever had finally broken. Frau Maria thanked God as she embraced her son, and Herman's friend, the shoemaker's daughter, squealed with delight.

"Margaret," Herman smiled weakly, "aren't you supposed to be in school?"

"That's the only good luck from the fire. The school burned down!"

"My wax tablet," moaned the boy.

"It surely melted," Margaret posited thoughtfully.

Herman closed his eyes again, but his face showed the strain of deep thought. Then he opened his eyes and spoke to his mother.

"I saw Our Lord in the fire, Mother, on His Cross! He held out His arms and the fire went back! If only I could have helped Him. If He would have taken me on the Cross with Him, together we could have stopped the fire from spreading."

Frau Maria cautioned her son about straining himself too much in his weakened condition. Was this the remnant of the fever speaking? she wondered. But his eyes had regained their brilliant clarity. Herman's mother knew that their light must have been rekindled by God Himself.

"If Christ takes me onto His Cross, then I will suffer a lot of pain," Herman struggled to continue. "But if I did it out of love, *love is strong!* The priest said that in his sermon the other day."

"Yes, Herman, love is strong," whispered his mother as she stroked his hair.

"I must go away then. I must go to a cloister. The priest said that love dwells there. Where shall I go, Mother?"

"Go where God calls you," she answered.

"In Sankt Mergen there was a canon from the Eifel. I think Steinfeld was the name of his cloister. He was a very good priest. Love surely must dwell there! Mother, when I am well, I will go to Steinfeld!"

Frau Maria's heart was pierced by an invisible sword as her son spoke. Whoever enters a cloister must leave everyone behind. However, she had presented her child as a gift to God and the Virgin Mary, and she knew that a mother's love must never impede her son from fulfilling his special calling from God.

"As God wills, Herman," she smiled painfully. "But there is still much time. You are very young."

"If you go to a cloister, then I will go with you, Joseph!" Margaret said.

"You must go to a nuns' cloister, Margaret; but not a noble one, because you don't have sixteen noble ancestors."

"Well, I will have to get them, then! Herman, the boys have been playing 'Crusade' on Martin Street. The burnt-down school is the Turkish castle where Stephen the Sultan lives. He has a wooden sword and wears a sheet around his head. He asked me to be his Sultana, but I told him I had to come visit you. Engelbert, Peter, and Arnold were throwing burnt turnips at him." When Margaret noticed the excitement in Herman's eyes upon hearing this story, she continued.

"And the Sultan sits on an old barrel and orders his Saracens to defend him. And they don't throw vegetables; they throw rocks!"

"If only I could be there Mother, I think I'm well again. May I get up?"

"No, Herman, you must stay in bed a few more days. You will be well soon enough. You must have patience."

"Oh, patience," the boy moaned. "Patience is the hardest virtue. Margaret, tell the crusaders to sneak through Geyer Street, then through the school master's pig pen and the back of the school. That way they'll catch the Sultan by surprise!"

"I'll go tell them now, Joseph. Goodbye!"

"Why does Margaret call you *Joseph*?" Herman's mother asked.

"Oh, that's a secret, Mother."

"A secret from your mother?"

Herman then decided to divulge his secret to her, provided that she promise not to share it with anyone else.

"Then your crusaders must not attack the Sultan and his Saracens. They must convert them!" Herman's mother remarked.

"I didn't think of that, Mother. But since Stephen has already been baptized, I don't think a few turnips will hurt him."

With that, the Crusade problem was solved, and Herman drifted back to sleep. An hour later, Margaret barged into the room and wanted to share the news of the victorious Crusade, but Frau Maria told her that she'd have to wait until tomorrow.

When the disappointed little girl had left, Frau Maria sat on the bed of her sleeping son and pondered the significance of his choosing to be called 'Joseph' and his vision of Christ among the flames. Then a premonition shook her soul: God had chosen this child for a higher calling and, as a consequence, for much suffering.

## Chapter Five
# The Bishop and the Donkey

**R**ainald von Dassel, archbishop of Cologne and chancellor to Emperor Frederick Barbarossa, tried to relax in his luxurious study in the new episcopal palace, which he built near the Hacht Gate. However, the news he was about to share with Gerhard, the overseer of the Church's possessions, made him anything but calm.

"I have been inspecting my estates for the past two weeks. I have also reviewed the accounts of your helpers, and what do you think I have found, Herr Gerhard?" the archbishop asked with a calm and even tone which belied his mood.

"I hope Your Grace has found everything in order," stammered the overseer.

"I will tell you what I have found," Archbishop Rainald said as he rose from his plush armchair and approached the quivering man. His voice rumbled, "Corruption and waste are what I have found! My mayors are filling their bellies at the peasants' expense! And, because they have squandered what they have stolen, they have had to mortgage lands and crops to the Jews, and their moneybags expand!

"They thought I was with Emperor Frederick in Italy, and they hoped the Milanese would kill me, and I would never return. But the unfortunate gentlemen miscalculated. Herr Gerhard, I have come home to sit in judgment over all of you!"

"Your Gracious Lordship!" stuttered the pallid Gerhard.

"I am not 'Your Gracious Lordship'. I am a very *ungracious* Lordship, and a *just* Lordship, Herr Gerhard!" Veins bulged from the bishop's forehead. "The mayors whose names you see listed here must render an account to me after the holidays. The property listed will then be turned over to the Cistercians of Kamp and Altenberg. They will maintain that land and turn over the income from it."

"But, Your Lordship, that is against all tradition!" objected the overseer.

"What good is your *tradition?* I prefer my lands to be properly managed. Go to Kamp and Altenberg and there you will see cloister lands that are managed to perfection. I know that the Cistercians oppose me because of my support for Pope Victor, but they can support Alexander all they want as long as they manage my property efficiently! Now go, and tell the Master of Ceremonies to come."

The overseer was happy to leave, and the archbishop fell back into his chair and relaxed. The tirade made him feel better, and just in time, too, because it was Christmas Eve, 1162. After a few moments, the Master of Ceremonies arrived.

"Lord Master of Ceremonies, what is the custom of Cologne on Christmas Eve?" inquired the archbishop.

"After Matins in the cathedral, Your Grace, your officials pull you in a cart to the Capitol church of Sankt Mergen. There you offer Midnight Mass. Afterward, you ride on a donkey supplied by the Sisters of Sankt Mergen to the Dawn Mass at Saint Cecilia's. The Mass of the Day is then celebrated in the cathedral."

"I am supposed to ride on a *donkey*?!" Archbishop Rainald asked indignantly. "Tell the Sisters to spare their beast the burden of the bishop. I will ride on my white stallion. That is more appropriate for the chancellor of the Holy Roman Empire."

"But, Your Grace, that goes against all tradition!" objected the Master of Ceremonies.

"You, too, come to me with your *tradition*," the bishop said disparagingly. "Your donkey and your tradition are a good match. You may go now."

The bishop returned to the papers covering his desk, and the Master of Ceremonies left, scratching his head.

\* \* \*

Twelve-year-old Herman carried an armful of hay to the stall of the donkey of Sankt Mergen. The animal greeted his arrival with a healthy bray.

"Eat your fill. Tonight you must carry Archbishop Rainald von Dassel. What an honor for you! You'll wear a white saddle, and all the people will look at you and the archbishop."

"The donkey will not be needed tonight!" interrupted Sister Iburga at the stable door. "The archbishop does not want to ride on him. He wants to ride on his stallion. The Master of Ceremonies just informed the abbess."

"That can't be, Sister! The archbishop of Cologne has always ridden on the donkey to Saint Cecilia's. This one must also do it!" Herman insisted.

"But he is not the true archbishop," declared the nun. "Pope Alexander has refused to confirm him, and Rainald doesn't want Victor to consecrate him. Victor is the one the emperor wants to put on Peter's throne."

"But there can be only one pope! And an unconsecrated bishop is worth nothing."

During this time of schism, division tore at the heart of the Church, and confusion clouded the minds of the faithful. One didn't know if a priestly blessing or consecration had come from hands that had been excommunicated. That is why people felt drawn as never before to the saints, who could provide guidance in such uncertain times. Christians visited the tombs and holy sites of the saints to secure a sense of certainty which, during this difficult period, even the papacy seemed to have failed to maintain.

Cologne had always honored her saints with abundant prayers and numerous artistic masterpieces. When Rainald von Dassel brought the marble shrine of the tombs of the Three Holy Kings from Milan the preceding summer, crowds of people came to Cologne to pray at the holy graves. Because of this, the city loved their bishop and supported Pope Victor, whom Rainald endorsed because of his allegiance to Emperor Frederick.

"The bishop must ride on the donkey!" Herman resolutely declared.

"Then you must go and tell him yourself," teased Sister Iburga.

"You're right, Sister. I *will* go to him! Have no fear my little gray friend. You will carry the archbishop!" He left the stall with such determined strides that Sister Iburga could not stop laughing as she pictured Herman storming into the "stall," as the bishop's new palace was now called.

\* \* \*

The doorkeeper at the archbishop's palace howled with laughter when the shabbily dressed youngster demanded to see the archbishop. "What do you want from the archbishop?" he finally managed to ask.

"It's very important. It's about the donkey!" Herman earnestly replied.

"If it has strayed, the archbishop cannot help you find it."

Herman offered a beautiful apple from Sister Iburga to the doorkeeper, who munched it with relish but refused to help the boy in return.

"Then I'll go alone!" shouted Herman, who was indignant over the man's deception. He scurried past the doorkeeper and ran down a long corridor until he heard a booming voice. He correctly assumed that only the archbishop would dare raise his voice here.

"You will immediately resign your office, Lord Abbot! Discipline, work, prayer, and sacrifice shall rule in my cloisters, not dissolution and worldly show. I am replacing you with someone who will fulfill your office properly and restore the cloister to God's favor where charity dwells. Now you may go!" The deposed abbot slipped through the door, and Herman immediately slid past him into the bishop's study. Though he faced a glaring, ominous presence, Herman stood calmly before the bishop.

"What do *you* want? And how did you get in here?!"

The terrified doorkeeper poked his head through the door just a moment too late. His fear rendered him speechless.

"Can't you spit out a word or two?" the bishop demanded.

"He's got my apple in his mouth... That's why he can't talk!" Herman remarked.

"Get out!" Rainald commanded the doorkeeper before he turned his attention to the boy. "How is it that you dare storm into my room unannounced?"

Herman looked up at the bishop with eyes of wonder but not fear. "I can dare to speak with God and go to Him at any time I want to," he cleverly said.

"Well, you certainly don't talk like a coward. My staff could use your courage. Now then, what do you want? I'm very busy. You know what day it is, don't you, little man?"

"That is why I came to see you, Your Grace. It's about the donkey."

"Yes?"

"You must ride on the donkey, not on your horse," Herman urged.

"And why must I?" asked the bishop with growing amusement.

"Our Lord also rode on a donkey. Twice even! On the flight to Egypt and on Palm Sunday. My mother said so, my teacher said so, and it's carved on the door of Sankt Mergen!"

"So?"

"So, if Jesus rode on a donkey, it isn't right for a bishop to ride on a horse on Christmas Eve!" The boy's eyes blazed as he finished.

The archbishop paced a few steps as he rubbed his chin with his fingers. This boy was certainly charming, but there was something even more than that. What he had said was true.

"I want to ask you another question, Your Grace," Herman continued.

"*Another* question?!" The bishop's eyes grew wider as he turned around to face the boy. Then he stooped down to eye level with Herman. "Ask it."

"Who is the true pope, Alexander or Victor?"

The chancellor immediately stood up and looked away from the courageous lad who dared to make such ingenuous yet piercing requests. He seemed to gather himself with great effort before responding.

"The true pope is he who stands with the Holy Roman Empire and its emperor! That is Pope Victor!" Rainald von Dassel caught himself trying too hard to sound convincing. He's just a child, the bishop thought as he drew a deep breath.

"You are not able to say that with certainty, Your Grace," Herman responded calmly. "Besides, the Holy Roman Empire was founded by men. The Holy Catholic Church was founded by Jesus, the God-Man. The emperor must stand with the pope, not the other way around."

"You are just a child! What do you understand about such things?!"

"Sister Iburga said you have not been consecrated yet," Herman continued. "And an unconsecrated bishop isn't worth much."

"I am the chancellor of the Empire," roared Rainald von Dassel. He wondered why he hadn't thrown this boy out earlier.

"What is a chancellor compared to a priest? You may be powerful on earth, but you are powerless in heaven. Your Grace, have yourself consecrated by the true pope!"

After an extended pause, the archbishop asked with a softened voice, "What is your name, my son?"

"Herman. I am the son of the cloth merchant Christopher, from Stephan Street."

"You are very poor, Herman."

"Of course. But I am happy about it, because poverty is holy."

"But you don't even have shoes! I'll give you some money to buy a pair."

"I don't want your gold, Lord Chancellor. Someone who is richer than you will give it to me when I need it."

"One who is richer than I? Who is this person?"

"The Blessed Virgin Mary. She has always helped me when I needed her."

Archbishop Rainald then remembered a strange report of what had happened to a child before the statue of the Madonna in Sankt Mergen. He wondered if this boy could be that child. Perhaps the Lord had sent him to speak to Rainald's ailing conscience. Although he led an exemplary life, Rainald's worldly ambition had impeded his spiritual growth. His accusing heart regularly reminded him of this. Perhaps if he could do some favor for this boy, God would calm his troubled soul.

"What is it you want me to do now?" he asked Herman.

"Please ride on the donkey tonight, Your Grace!"

"Is that all? Nothing for yourself?"

"Yes, Your Grace, you can help me," responded Herman after a moment's reflection. "I want to go to the cloister of the Premonstratensian canons at Steinfeld. But my father says we are too poor to pay for my board. My father has regained his health, but we are still very poor."

"I will help you, my boy," the bishop assured him. "Your father will not refuse the aid of the archbishop. But I have one request."

"What is that, Your Grace?"

"Please pray for me!" urged the bishop in a plaintive tone as he felt his gaze drawn to the boy.

"Oh, I will surely do that! I will do that every day! I will pray for your happy death and salvation!" The boy's eyes smiled reassuringly at the archbishop, who rang his silver bell and ordered an attendant to send in the Master of Ceremonies once again.

"My dear Master of Ceremonies, the old tradition will remain," said the bishop. "I will ride on the donkey from Sankt Mergen to Saint Cecilia's tonight."

\* \* \*

Hundreds of candles burning in Sankt Mergen's choir loft seemed to flicker to the sonorous tones of the organ and the canonesses' sacred chant of the Midnight Mass. The bishop sat in his choir stall with his face buried in his hands. Herman's face beamed as he knelt with the other servers and prayed from the depths of his heart for his benefactor.

After the High Mass, the donkey was led to the bishop. The ancient tradition also required the prioress to present to the bishop a silk purse with three gold pieces, the fat sister dean to give him a pair of gloves, and the sister treasurer a wax candle. The bishop's face clouded over when he saw his mount, but then he espied the boy in the crowd nodding joyfully. The bishop smiled in return and climbed into the white saddle.

"Yeeaaah!" brayed the jackass, causing the crowd to erupt with jubilation as the archbishop rode to St. Cecilia's.

## Chapter Six
# The Luminous River

The following year was one of special graces for Herman because he was preparing to receive his First Holy Communion. The pastor of Saint Martin's helped prepare Herman and his young classmates for this great event. This particular year brought other changes in Herman, who was now spending much more time in serious reflection. In fact, his parents grew concerned that he was becoming too quiet.

One beautiful spring day, Herman and two other boys sat on the bank of the Rhine River. They dangled their legs in the water and poured forth the words of their conversation into the ebb and flow of the river's currents.

"Did you know that there's gold in this water?" Stephen asked. "Hundreds of years ago, a king threw his treasure into this river. Golden goblets and crowns and jewelry are all still sitting down there. Some nights you can see them shining from the deep."

"Have you ever seen it, Sultan?" asked Herman.

"Not yet, Herman, but I've tried several times. I still haven't given up hope, though. And when I do see those treasures, I'll dive in and get them. Then I'll be wealthier than the archbishop, and I'll build the most beautiful palace in Cologne!"

"Sure you will, Stephen," mocked Peter, a red-haired boy with fiery locks who was as mischievous as he looked.

"There *is* gold in the Rhine, Peter. Look at the merchant ships that are constantly passing by. Do you see how low that ship lies in the water? That means it's loaded with fine silk and carpet and spice and other luxuries. When I grow up, I will fill a ship with riches, and they will fill my sacks with money." Eagerly the boy looked at the trading ship which, heavily laden, sailed past down the Rhine.

"Forget that miserable trading ship!" Peter said. "For all I care it can sink with its cinnamon and silk. If only it was a *Viking* ship, with a blood red dragon! They sailed down the Rhine a couple hundred years ago and wherever they went they left behind burning towns and villages. That was the life! Adventure is better than gold. Besides, Stephen, I could steal your vast treasures, and then where would you be? I want to ride with Berthold, the mad outlaw who goes with his men through Bavaria destroying everything in his way."

When Stephen spat on the ground, Peter sneered, "You don't have the courage and strength to lead that kind of life. *That's* living!"

"That's not living," Herman said. "That's not noble or courageous or strong."

"What do you mean? Many noblemen lead that kind of life," Peter retorted.

"A title doesn't make someone noble. His heart makes him noble." Now Herman's eyes blazed with inspiration. "It is not noble to kill defenseless people. That takes no courage."

"So what *is* noble, wise Solomon?"

Herman thought a long time before answering. The rays of the setting sun shone on the river as he softly spoke. "Life calls for true greatness and nobility! *That's* real living!"

"What do you mean, *true greatness and nobility*, wise Solomon?" Peter asked sarcastically.

Herman looked quietly at the river, which now began to glow in shades of deep red. "Do you see how the water sparkles?" he asked his comrades.

"Golden treasure!" cried Stephen.

"Viking fire!" shouted Peter.

"*NO!* Something entirely different: true greatness and nobility." He continued to address the two quizzical faces. "In the Rhine flows the blood of the saints! St. Gereon and his soldiers who were murdered at Mechtern. And the blood of Saint Ursula and her maidens who were martyred. *That* is true nobility. That is *life!*"

"You poor fool. To let yourself to be killed is anything but life."

"Unless it is for the sake of Christ, Peter."

"Well, what if there are no heathens around to kill you?"

"Then to *live* for the sake of Christ!" said Herman with deep conviction. He stood up and his face was shining from the reflection of the sun. "I believe that true greatness is not found in external things, like the Rhine or the forest. True nobility is found *within* us. Yes, that is where true greatness must really be."

Herman didn't mind Peter's sarcastic words or Stephen's dubious looks. He also knew that true greatness was not easily discouraged by opposition but rather strengthened by grace to overcome it. As if he were dreaming, he stared at the shimmering water. "That is holiness and true nobility. That is life!" his lips whispered once more, almost inaudibly. Then he walked quietly in the direction of the Cathedral, from which the flag with the three crowns waved.

The other two boys were likewise silent all of a sudden. They looked after their strange comrade, over whose head the three crowns shone high above. Then, without another word, they separated and went home.

That night, as Stephen was snoring and peacefully dreaming of sacks of gold, Peter had trouble sleeping for the first time in his life. For hours he lay there and stared into the darkness. What Herman had said about true greatness really bothered the boy who had known only violence and struggle throughout his young life. Peter was also preparing for First Holy Communion, but the pastor's lessons had not inspired him as they had Herman, because Peter often daydreamed about the days of the Vikings during religion class. On this night, for the first time, something completely different entered his mind, and would not leave it. Again and again he saw Herman, in the glow of the sun and water, speaking about true nobility and holiness, about life and the true greatness which are found not outside, but within.

Peter futilely tried to convince himself that Herman was just imitating the pastor, but his young heart gave him no rest. So he resolved to ask his classmate more about God's heroes.

"Herman," the boy said the next morning, "you know I was only joking yesterday about the Vikings and Berthold. Sometime I would like to hear more about Gereon and his soldiers."

"I am certainly too wild for you," Peter continued hesitantly to the beaming boy, "but if you would be my friend, we could help each other. You can tell me your stories, and I'll fight for you whenever you need it!"

He extended a dirty hand to Herman, who accepted it and shook it vigorously saying, "Peter, you're all right!"

During their free time, the two friends explored the crypts of churches, seeking out those old magnificent chapels under the churches of the Apostles, of Sankt Mergen and St. Gereon. They

41

both loved how the feeble glow of the hanging vigil lights heightened the mood of ancient mystery among the ponderous pillars, between which lay the stone tombs of the martyrs. Palms and crowns were chiseled in them.

"This is it! True greatness and nobility!" Herman whispered to his friend with awe, then reached for the hand of his friend. "Here is life!"

Herman later explained to Peter that "crypt" meant "hidden." "True greatness and holiness are hidden within things, hidden under other appearances, perhaps. Just like the consecrated host, Peter. It is God hidden under the appearance of bread."

Herman often daydreamed about the impending, miraculous wellspring that would burst forth within his soul on the day of his First Holy Communion. "Christ is life!" the priest had said. Therefore, Life Himself would reside in the crypt of his heart.

"Peter, it is so immeasurably great!" Herman would suddenly exclaim in the midst of his joyous reflection. Peter did not understand much of what his friend said, but he admired Herman's zeal, the strength of which shone forth in his bright eyes.

Herman constantly reflected on Christ's words, "I am the Life!" Now he saw all life from a different perspective. Everything contained something inside, invisible to the eye. And within this crypt dwelt God, Eternal Life Itself.

Herman could not contain his anger once when he saw a boy rip a rose from its stem, throw it to the ground, and step on it.

"You're stamping out life!" Herman cried.

"What is a rose?" the boy asked.

"It is something living, and all life comes from God."

Herman now perceived God's breath in every creature. A great respect for all living things, and a love of silence and solitude, in which he found the way of true greatness and life, grew more and more within his heart. He developed an even deeper love for Mary. His prayers to her grew more personal and fervent as he came to see in Her the Mother who bore Life itself in her arms.

The day of First Holy Communion drew near and the prayers of the boy became ever more fervent. It seemed to Herman that an overpowering, luminous river was breaking into his soul. And the river carried him away, overpowered his young soul and bore it into the sea of Life. As if from far away he heard the words of St. Augustine:

> *Where is there room in me into which God can come? Where can God come to me, God Who created heaven and earth? O Lord, my God, is there something in me which could hold You? But do heaven and earth hold You, which You created and in which limits You have created me? The house of my soul into which You desire to come is narrow. Make it wide! It is fragile. Build it anew!*

Herman completely immersed himself in Eternal Love as he received his Savior in Holy Communion for the first time. The profound joy of this experience made him want to cry out in pain from the holy wound he bore in his heart.

The day of his First Holy Communion was momentous for another reason. After a prolonged hesitation in spite of the wishes of the archbishop, Christopher finally gave his son permission to enter the Premonstratensian cloister at Steinfeld.

Herman left home that autumn. Difficult indeed was the farewell to his home, his parents, the Blessed Virgin of Sankt Mergen and the city with the three crowns.

"May the Holy Mother protect you!" exclaimed Frau Maria in tears, kissing her child tenderly.

"Just wait, Joseph, I'll surely follow you, you'll see," promised his dear friend Margaret.

Herman did not have many words. He left the walls of Cologne behind and soon broad plains surrounded him and the land grew quieter as he drew closer to the hilly region of the Eifel.

The boy, however, looked happily at the distant heights. He knew that there, over the hills, silence waited for him, and in its depths he would find God and life.

## Chapter Seven
# Steinfeld

**A**n autumn storm raged over the Eifel hills.  The fierce wind chased the clouds, scattering them across the sky like a wolf scattering a flock of sheep.  It shook the pines and firs, and stripped the colorful leaves from the birch and linden trees.  It also battered the little pilgrim Herman, who was climbing the final, steep approach to the abbey of Steinfeld.  Perhaps this wild companion wind of the Eifel was an unbaptized heathen at heart, since it pulled so hard at Herman's jacket, that it seemed to want to hold him back with all its strength from his vocation.  But the small boy of Cologne resisted the powerful wind with all his might and climbed the last hill, out of breath.

Herman was exhausted from the long and difficult journey as well as from lack of sleep.  He had spent the previous night in a haystack in Zulpich, but the howling storm and wolves kept him from sleeping soundly.  At least his destination was now in sight.  The two mighty monastery towers loomed overhead, rising into the sky like strong bulwarks of God.  This was his new home!  In this holy place he would find the true greatness and nobility which he sought with all his heart: the hidden life of the spirit.

As Herman entered the monastery's massive outer gate, several huge dogs sprang upon him.  They almost buried the boy until a shrill whistle called them off.  The dismayed youth saw that he had been saved by a member of the Order, who was leading a magnificent horse into the stable.

"Brother Eberhard, what kind of horse is that?" asked an old canon who approached with the aid of a cane.

"A splendid four-year-old, Father Abbot," the brother answered with pride.  "There is not one like it in the entire cloister stable.  It has strong bones, fetlocks, and good teeth," he said, exposing the horse's teeth to the abbot who nodded his approval.

"Where did we get this fine horse?" he asked.

"It was willed to us by one of the tenants of the monastery.  His wife just brought it."

"Then I won't have it," the abbot responded sharply.  "His wife will be in poverty.  Take the horse back right away."

"Yes, Your Reverence," Eberhard said immediately but with obvious disappointment.

Finally noticing Herman, the abbot asked, "What do you want, young man? You're in the way here!"

"I want to become a canon in your cloister," said Herman, gazing into the old abbot's ice-gray eyes. "I am Herman. My father's name is Christopher, of Cologne."

The old priest's eyes softened, but he disregarded the hand which the youth extended with uncertainty. "We shall see if we can use you." Then he entered the stable, from which Eberhard was bringing out a saddle.

"Are you new here?" Eberhard asked Herman cheerfully. "Come, sit on this horse. You can ride with me to return it to the farmer's wife."

Herman delightedly mounted the steed, but at that very moment the abbot came out of the stable.

"The stables have to be cleaned out, Brother Eberhard!" ordered the approaching abbot. "What's this, young man? You haven't come here to take rides. Get down from there and take this pitchfork. Use it to clean out the dung from the stable. Brother Eberhard will help you when he returns."

The crimson-faced Herman quickly dismounted and seized the pitchfork. He had never cleaned a stable before. He'd only fed the Sisters' donkey, not cleaned its stall. After only a few minutes of working in the fetid, steaming straw, Herman grew fatigued and squeamish.

"Throw it more to the side there!" ordered the abbot. "Otherwise you'll have to climb over a pile of dung to get out. Do it properly, and don't waste time, young man!" Then the abbot turned away and went back into the cloister.

Herman pitched with all his strength, though he was very tired and hungry. He had dreamed of Steinfeld as a place of supreme holiness, but no one seemed concerned about his weakened condition. Instead, the abbot had pressed into his hands this odious pitchfork. Herman wondered what stables and pitchforks and dung had to do with true greatness and nobility.

Brother Eberhard returned over an hour later to find a sweaty boy with trembling arms. He also saw that the stable had been cleaned out.

"You've done a good job, boy" he said. "Much better than I expected from a city boy. You must be tired from all the work and travel."

"Brother, I didn't come here to pitch dung," groaned Herman, wiping his brow with his sleeve. "The abbot certainly is a strict man!"

"That's for sure. And there are many other harsh storms here in the Eifel," laughed Eberhard. "But you'll come to understand soon, and then you'll feel at home here."

Herman looked outside the stable door at the stern towers growing darker against the dusky clouds. He wondered if he would ever feel at home in this place. Home was Cologne, Mother and Father, Sister Iburga and Margaret. The growing emptiness within him almost brought him to tears, but he fought them back with other thoughts.

"Brother, don't you ever get hungry here?" Herman asked.

"Of course. Hungry as a wolf! It won't be long before the bell rings for dinner. Go now to the Brother Porter with your bundle. He'll guide you further."

The Brother Porter ordered Herman to wash up before he was assigned a place to sleep. "You smell like a stable. Go at once to the cloister washing-cell. You'll see that one of the brothers carved the heads of cats on the wash basin. Cats are clean animals. So clean yourself thoroughly, my boy."

Herman washed himself vigorously, though he had little energy to admire the beauty of the masonry on the huge stone washbasin. Then he heard the dinner bell ring, and he saw the canons pass by on their way to the refectory. Their white habits heightened Herman's awareness of his own dirty condition. The cloister students followed, their young, ruddy faces contrasting with their white habits. They, too, proceeded silently and solemnly with their hands folded under their scapulars.

Herman quickly dried himself and hurried to catch up to the cloister students. He could smell the food as he approached the entrance to the refectory. Then he felt a powerful hand seize him by the collar. It was the abbot.

"You have not visited the church yet. Go there immediately! You have much to say to Our Lord and to His Holy Mother upon your entrance into religious life."

One of the brothers silently escorted Herman to the abbey church. He knelt before the tabernacle and prayed the *Our Father*, and his request for "our daily bread" was more fervent than ever before. Then, kneeling before the beautiful old statue of the Blessed Virgin, Herman prayed the *Hail Mary*. Afterward, the only prayer he could say was, "Dear Mother of God, please let the abbot know how hungry I am!"

His escort finally led Herman to the refectory, where he was assigned a place at one of the cloister students' tables. After saying grace, Herman devoured a large bowl of soup and a giant piece of bread. He did not notice his surroundings until he had satisfied the worst of his hunger.

The priests sat at the long head table, at the head of which sat the abbot. Next to him sat a priest with a lively, good-natured face, who Herman later learned was the prior. The other canons sat according to age. The brothers sat at the second table, and Herman noticed Brother Eberhard, who acknowledged the boy with a smile. At the upper end of the next table sat the grave and respectable *quadrivium* students, and at the lower end sat the little *trivium* students who did not seem nearly as pious. They cast curious looks at Herman, especially one straw-haired boy, who kept nudging his neighbor and pointing at Herman. Perhaps it was his enormous appetite that was so amusing.

Herman's stomach and eyes had been so preoccupied that he did not even notice that someone was reading from a book. A canon was reading in what must have been Latin, because Herman recognized a few of the words from church. He asked his neighbor to the right what was being read.

"Don't you know? *Vita Sancti Norberti (The Life of St. Norbert).*"

"Do you understand what he's reading?!"

"Every word."

Herman groaned. He had so much catching up to do. The other boys were so much smarter than he. Then Herman's neighbor to his left told him that none of the *trivium* students understood a word of what was being read. He also cautioned Herman about the abbot's using a rod on any boy caught talking during meals.

Night prayer in the church followed the meal and everyone went quietly to rest. Herman was so tired that he failed to notice how hard the dormitory bed was. He heard another autumn storm beating against the shutters. Then he slept.

## Chapter Eight
# Saint Augustine and the Bats

When Herman attended class the next morning with the other *trivium* students, he discovered that his classmates were not nearly as advanced as he thought. Their teacher, Father Fridolin, constantly corrected the boys' errors in Latin pronunciation and verb conjugations. Conrad, the boy who claimed he understood "every word" of the Latin biography of Saint Norbert, became so muddled in the declensions that the entire class erupted with laughter. The stern teacher, however, quickly quelled the disturbance.

Herman approached Conrad later at recreation and said, "Last night you told me that you understood every word the priest was reading."

"Do you doubt that, little man?" Conrad asked menacingly.

"I have faith in the Gospel, not in you, Conrad," Herman replied.

"What do you know about faith, you worldling?" Conrad poked Herman on the chest and then pushed him into a group of other *triviums*. "You probably haven't even been baptized yet. Hey, everybody, let's baptize this poor heathen!"

A howling gang of half a dozen boys overpowered the defenseless newcomer. They seized Herman and dragged him to the washing cell where the excited band of boys lifted Herman up and threw him into the immense wash basin. They dunked him a couple of times before finally allowing him to climb out. When the boys started dancing around their dripping-wet victim, Herman snapped. He approached Conrad, fully prepared to punch him in the nose. Just then, a *quadrivium* student entered the washing cell.

"Herman! You are to go immediately to see the abbot!"

"To the abbot?!" coughed the boy. "I can't go like this!"

"When the abbot says immediately, he means it!"

The other boys froze when they heard the word *abbot*. They backed away from Herman, hoping he wouldn't tell the abbot what had happened. If he did, the abbot would most likely cancel the "student-abbot holiday" on the feast of the Holy Innocents. This particular day was the highlight of their year.

\* \* \*

Herman entered Abbot Ulrick's cell and found the canon hunched over his desk reading what must have been an important letter. He was so absorbed in his letter that it was a long time before he even noticed the dripping-wet boy. He reacted with a strange jerk of his body and a twitch of his face. Herman knew he was doomed. What he didn't know was that the abbot himself had been given the very same treatment when he had entered Steinfeld, and that the abbot back then conducted the same examination which Ulrick was now going to give to Herman. He was curious to see how the boy would stand up to the test.

"How is it that you are wet?" he asked severely.

"I, uh, I, uh, I fell into the water," stammered Herman.

"Rather, someone pushed you in, correct? ...Did you hear my question?!" thundered Ulrick.

Herman raised his head and looked imploringly at his stern superior, who wiped his mouth with a handkerchief to hide any trace of a smile.

"You seem to be a very awkward lad to simply fall into water. Do you have any other clothes?"

Herman shook his head, "No."

"Go to Brother William. He will give you a habit. You may wear it until your clothes dry, but then you must take it off. The habit of the Norbertine Order is a sacred garment which must be earned."

Herman blushed. For the very first time, he would be permitted to wear the white habit.

"Then, go to the north tower," the abbot ordered. "Above the Chapel of Saint Michael is the library. There, on the second shelf on the right, in the lowest corner, are the works of Saint Augustine. Bring me the first volume."

"Yes, Your Reverence."

"One more thing. In the arches of the tower there are nested all kinds of birds, bats, and owls. Go and drive them out."

"Yes, Your Reverence."

So, clothed in the beautiful white habit, Herman climbed the stairs of the fortified tower. He entered the library, where bookshelves covered the walls from floor to ceiling. Most of the titles were written in Latin. Herman thought that the abbot must have read all these works because he was so wrinkled and bent and ill humored. After an exhaustive search, Herman finally found the pigskin volume of Saint Augustine and proceeded to ascend the tower stairs.

The narrow, twisting steps were also very steep. Herman firmly gripped the rope which hung above his left shoulder in place of a fixed banister. It was so dark that he couldn't even see his left hand. Herman grew dizzy and his heart began to pound.

Finally, he saw an oblique ray of light fall upon the stairway above him. Then there was another ascent into darkness. A second ray of light sliced the darkness. Herman climbed out onto a broad window bank for some much-needed air. The wind rustled his hair as he leaned outside and gazed at the scenic view before him.

The hills, moors and meadows of the Eifel lay before the somber, black forests of fir trees. In the distance, Herman saw the seven mountains, behind which was the city of Bonn-on-the-Rhine. Then he saw his own city, Cologne, very far away. He wondered what his mother and father were doing at that moment. When he thought of Sister Iburga, he could almost see the church tower of Sankt Mergen in the deepening twilight. There, back in Sankt Mergen, stood the altar of the Blessed Virgin, to whom he had once given an apple.

Everything at home was so different from the cloister of Steinfeld. His first two days had been filled with so much trouble; it had been nothing like he anticipated. First, there was the abbot and the pitchfork, and then the "baptism" by his classmates. Now he had to clear out the bats and birds from the terrifying tower where they were sure to return anyway.

Herman wondered if it would be better for him to return home. Perhaps it was a sign from God. Then his face was hit with a blast of what Brother Eberhard called that "stubborn" Eifel wind. It filled him with another thought: Yes, conditions had been severe, but had they been rough enough to defeat him?

"No!" he yelled out the window. "I'm no longer a child! I'll overcome it!" Then he hastened up the last steps to the top of the tower.

Nearly every niche in the arches was home to a flying animal. Owls stared reproachfully from their dark nooks, and bats hung from every beam, sleeping with their heads buried in their wings. Suddenly, one fluttered through the vault, grazing Herman's head. Fear and repulsion nearly paralyzed him, but he remembered his resolution. He firmly clenched his jaw, as he gripped the pigskin volume he would use to drive the birds to flight. As he began, the vault resounded with the cries and fluttering of the frightened creatures. Herman persisted through his fear, and finally cleared the belfry of every winged creature.


Herman returned to the abbot's cell with a badly soiled habit. The abbot was finishing a letter when the boy entered. He handed the letter to a messenger and sent him away with a sharp message: "Tell the archbishop I cannot fulfill his request for one of my brothers to manage an estate of his. He can have whatever he wants from my stables of sheep, oxen, and horses, but I will not give him a brother. On Judgment Day I will not have to give an account of my animals, but I will of the members of the Order! Now go!"

The messenger bowed silently before departing. Then the abbot turned to Herman.

"Have you driven those birds and bats from the tower?"

"Yes, Your Reverence."

"*All* of them?"

"Yes, Your Reverence."

Ulrick approached the boy and put his hands over Herman's heart and head.

"Have you also driven them out from here?" he gently asked.

The boy blushed deeply but then nodded vigorously. Then the old, wrinkled face of the abbot brightened.

"Good! You've driven them out using Saint Augustine! Yes, lad, in this book there is much light to drive out the darkness. It has helped me many times to drive those winged creatures of darkness out of the tower."

Herman laughed when he imagined the old abbot climbing up the tower to drive out the bats. Then he thought about what his superior really meant. The abbot looked at Herman and extended his hand for the first time. The boy took it and shook it heartily.

"Well done, my son. You may go now."


Ulrick smiled to himself after Herman left. He was pleased that this lad had passed the test. Then he reclined in his chair and opened the volume of Saint Augustine.

Herman felt very different as he walked through the cloister garden. Everything seemed like home to him now that the abbot had accepted him.

"Have you driven the birds out of the tower?" called Brother Eberhard as he led two yellow Eifel oxen out to the fields. "I saw them flying around up there."

"Yes. I got them out with that thick book of Saint Augustine. The abbot said that was the right thing to use."

"Indeed, he's right. Now come here and let me help you get those spider webs off that habit."

Conrad and the *triviums* greeted Herman when he returned.

"What a fine baptismal garment you have!" Conrad said.

"It certainly is," laughed Herman.

"Did you tell on us?"

"I'm no tattletale!"

"No, you're a good guy. You fit in here. We'll be friends, if you want to." And, for the second time that day, Herman happily accepted and shook an offered hand.

## Chapter Nine
# Saint Michael's Sword

**T**he *trivium* students of Steinfeld swept the fallen leaves of late September into a giant golden and russet pile. Their laughter echoed throughout the cloister courtyard as they worked with determination and zeal. Tomorrow was not only a feastday. It was also the day on which the new chapel of Saint Michael would be dedicated. In addition to its spiritual joys, a feastday such as this called for something special, prepared by the Brother Cook.

"Perhaps he's making something from the calf which Brother Eberhard took to the Brother Butcher," speculated the corpulent Arnulf.

"Today red, tomorrow dead," sighed the melancholy Anthony.

"The calf?"

"No, silly! The leaves! Yesterday they hung from the trees; today they have beautiful colors; tomorrow, they're rubbish."

"*Sic transit gloria mundi*" ("*So passes the glory of the world*"), quoted the erudite Albert.

"You owl!" shouted Conrad. "You talk like Gertrude, the old hermitess of Duvenforest. The '*gloria mundi*' ('*glory of this world*') is just beginning for us! Someday I'm going to be archbishop of Cologne or an abbot in Bohemia. Then you will have to bow down before me!"

Conrad leapt up to the top of the giant leaf pile, spewing leaves in his wake. Then he raised his broom with great majesty, as if it were a crosier. His reign was short-lived, however. The others pulled Conrad down from his pedestal in a leafy mutiny, and, in a moment, the *triviums* were playfully undoing the results of their hard work. The glorious, golden pile was animated with twisting limbs and bodies. Then Father Fridolin entered the courtyard.

He grabbed a broom and began to swing indiscriminately at the pile. In a moment's time, the boys untangled themselves and stood before their teacher, straightening their clothes and rubbing their wounds. The last to emerge from the leaves was the only one wearing secular clothing. Herman looked at his teacher with such a joyful sparkle that the priest could not conceal the hint of a smile. The class responded with a hearty burst of laughter that resounded throughout the courtyard.

"You still have worldly foolishness in your head, Herman. You seem to have been the instigator, so come along with me. The rest of you sweep up these leaves again. In the tower, Herman, you can reflect on the proper behavior for a cloister student."

"I was the one who started it!" Conrad spoke up. "Herman was the last to join in."

"You were not asked!" Father Fridolin responded sharply.

The priest escorted Herman across the courtyard to the north tower, where he was locked inside the library. The teacher left the boy a book and told him to read it for a couple of hours. The birds began to return to the "tower" of Herman's head, as he reflected on the injustice of the false accusation. However, he soon realized that these two hours provided him something for which he had been yearning: solitude. The birds circled the tower before flying away. Herman opened the book: *The Life of the Venerable Archbishop Norbert of Xanten.*

\* \* \*

Meanwhile, Father Fridolin stood before the abbot, who shrugged when he heard the teacher confess that he might have been strict to the point of being unjust.

"Nonsense!" growled Ulrick. "Was he defiant or rebellious?"

"No, Your Reverence, just very downhearted."

"That doesn't matter," smiled the abbot. "Our cloister is not a convent but rather an army camp! 'Steinfeld' means 'stone field,' and a field of stones it is. The hand which clears this land cannot be soft. I also need soldiers who can travel east from Steinfeld to the mission territories of Bohemia and Moravia. The sons of Norbert must be soldiers who can endure many hard battles!

"I received a letter from Abbot Gezo saying that one of our cloisters in Bohemia is suffering from a lack of discipline. Abbot Reiner is too feeble to restore order, so I will have to do it. That is why I must test, and test very hard, the young men who wish to wear the venerable habit of the Premonstratensian Order!"

The teacher nodded silently. He knew that Abbot Ulrick was right.

\* \* \*

During this time, Herman was absorbed in the life-story of the founder of the Norbertine Order. He was surprised to read about the stormy youth of the noble Norbert of Xanten, but he found great inspiration in the power of God's grace, which converted Norbert.

Norbert traveled barefoot through Germany to spread the Gospel, even in winter. He derived much grace and strength from his mortification, grace and strength that he needed to serve in his challenging post as archbishop of Magdeburg.

One severe trial occurred when a slanderous rumor was circulated throughout Magdeburg alleging that Archbishop Norbert had stolen sacred relics and was preparing to flee the city with them. When Norbert's friends saw the rage of the people, they hid him in the tower of the old cathedral, where he sang Matins of the feast of Saint Paul.

The people launched a siege of the tower. After assailing the cathedral all night, a few men were able to scale the wall and enter the tower. With swords drawn, they rushed inside to fulfill their deadly mission. But when Norbert fearlessly met them, dressed in his purple vestments, these men fell to the ground and begged for forgiveness.

Another group of men rushed upon the scene and, believing that the archbishop had already been killed, they attacked the chancellor. Norbert offered himself to these men to avoid further bloodshed. The same man who stabbed the chancellor then attacked Norbert. The sword glanced off Norbert's shoulder, smearing it with the chancellor's blood, which can still be seen on the ancient vestment. The next day, Norbert celebrated a Mass of thanksgiving for his deliverance.

"That's it! That's true greatness and nobility!" Herman's voice echoed through the library. The punishment he had received had also been a blessing. Then he felt a hand on his shoulder.

"Your time is over. You can go now," said Father Fridolin.

"*Already*? What a shame." Herman closed the book.

"Our founder is a great saint, don't you think, Herman?"

Herman only nodded, but the priest saw the glow in his eyes. It brightened into a radiant smile when he told the young man that he could serve the High Mass the next day and even swing the censer.

"The censer?!" Herman exclaimed, joyfully incredulous that a bad situation had so quickly turned good.

"Then you can ask Saint Michael the Archangel to help you become a strong son of Saint Norbert."

\* \* \*

Great rejoicing resounded throughout the church the next morning. Herman stood before the newly-dedicated altar swinging the censer. The morning rays of sunlight which shone through the windows seemed to ignite Saint Michael's sword as the *Te Deum* rang out:

> *We praise You, O God. We acclaim You, Lord and Master.*
> *Everlasting Father, all the earth bows down before You.*
> *All the angels sing Your praise.*
> *The hosts of heaven and the angelic powers,*
> *All the cherubim and seraphim call out to You in unending*
> *chorus.*

Saint Michael's sword shone with a brilliant intensity that amazed Herman. In his own mind's eye, a fire had begun to rage outside the windows of the cloister church. As huge flames licked the sides of the new church, Herman tried to scream, but no sound came from his white lips. He wondered why no one else saw the fire, and he felt a searing heat scorch his heart. It seemed as though Saint Michael had ignited the entire cloister with his fiery sword, yet the canons and students continued their sacred chant, uniting heaven and earth in one jubilant song:

> *Holy, holy, holy is the Lord God of angel hosts.*
> *The heavens and the earth are filled, Lord,*
> *With Your majesty and glory.*

When the last strains of the *Te Deum* faded away, Herman saw the fire die out as well. Everything returned to normal. Herman, however, knew that he had seen a tiny bit of eternal light, power, and love, uniting heaven and earth and consuming the cloister and his own heart in immortal flames.

\* \* \*

Christmas was over, but the *trivium* class grew very excited about the approaching feast of the Holy Innocents, the day on which the cloister observed the holiday of the "student-abbot." Conrad would be abbot, Anthony prior, and the fat Arnulf subprior. The *triviums* had decided this by vote in anticipation of the day. During Vespers on the preceding day, the words of the *Magnificat* were sung:

*He has cast down the mighty from their thrones,*
*And has exalted the lowly.*

Then the cantor relinquished his staff, the symbol of his authority, to a student who then directed the canticle to its conclusion. The canonry's entire routine for the next day was changed. At the Divine Office, the *triviums* sat in the choir stalls of the priests, and the priests sat in the boys' places. Conrad sat on the abbot's throne, reigning for one day over all of Steinfeld. He looked very solemn and recollected during Mass, but he was really concentrating on his plans for the day.

The priests exchanged places with the students in the refectory, too. There 'Abbot' Conrad strictly enforced the rule of silence. When he noticed Father Fridolin whispering to his neighbor, he banished both of them to the north tower to clear out the bats.

Later that day, Abbot Conrad presided over the Chapter of Faults. Although he showed mercy to Abbot Ulrick on account of his advanced years, he ordered Father Fridolin to receive a dozen whacks with a rod for unjustly punishing Herman for the leaf pile incident. The priest accepted the judgment with great humility.

Abbot Conrad then ordered the brother cook to step forward. Trembling, the cook approached the judgment seat.

"Brother Cook, you are accused of watering down the soup. You shall now see how water tastes! The gallon tankard which you 'secretly' fill with beer will be filled with water, and you will empty it before our eyes," Abbot Conrad commanded.

Conrad ignored the brother's plea for clemency and forced him to empty the container. The brother cook finally finished and wobbled away. Then Abbot Conrad issued his final decree:

"Come forward, venerable frater Herman. It is not right that you should walk through our cloister dressed as a child of the world. You have proven yourself worthy of wearing the habit of the Norbertine Order. Therefore, you will be vested in it immediately!"

And so Herman was.


Herman's joy increased the next day when the real abbot, Ulrick, did not repeal the order of his 'predecessor.' He rather gave thanks to God for exalting the humble on the feast of the Holy Innocents.

## Chapter Ten

# Mary's Dam

The abbey of Mariëngaarde was a daughter house of Steinfeld, located in Frisian lands that bordered the North Sea. The Frisians, who called it the "sea of death," waged an almost continual battle against the ocean every year to preserve the scanty soil of their homeland. The lonely farms of Halligen and their neighboring peasant houses among the marshes and moors were especially dependent upon the local dam to save them from the encroaching sea.

That is why, in the cold winter of 1164, Abbot Frederick insisted that the farmers walk with him to the ocean where he pointed to the shoreline and said:

"Men, when the spring storms arrive, ice will pound against our dam. It is not strong enough to protect us. We must build the dam higher and wider."The men grumbled about doing such work in the middle of winter, but the abbot enforced the ancient Frisian law, which decreed that whoever did not work must leave the territory. Then Frederick and his Norbertines led the men in the arduous task. The canons set an example not only of piety but also of diligence.

\* \* \*

Four months earlier, Abbot Ulrick had sent his young confreres to the newly founded Frisian cloister to complete their studies. Here they could learn to pray and work as never before. Abbot Frederick, the prior, and Father Fridolin gave the future priests little time to rest. When improvements on the dam were finished, work in the swamps and moors would begin.

Even the strongest of the men grew exhausted from working the frozen earth, but they continued to fortify the dam. When the work was finished, the abbot consecrated the dam to Our Lady. Then the spring storms began to whip the North Sea, dashing its heavy waves against the walls of the dam. The peasants in their huts lit blessed candles before the image of Mary and prayed for her protection over the dam consecrated to her. They prayed also for blessings upon Abbot Frederick, the man whose foresight had fortified Mary's dam. Its strength would soon be tested.

* * *

The peasants could hear the clanging of the Matins bell despite the howl of the raging storm. The bell was calling the canons and students to the church for the midnight Office, but to the villagers, the bell rang out as a promise of heavenly protection. Calloused hands were soon folded in prayer. Even the youngest of the brothers realized the dangers of the stormy night.

"Hold your hand over the dam, Mother," Herman prayed with confidence. The dam would not break because Our Lady was protecting it. The now tall fourteen-year-old had indeed grown more mature and manly, but his faith in Jesus and Mary remained childlike.

The Norbertines were distracted from their prayers by hammer-like blows to the cloister door. The words of the psalms faltered on their quivering lips. Then the canon on night watch entered the church, approached the abbot, and whispered to him. The abbot immediately rose, but he signaled the others to continue praying as he walked with calm steps out of the church. The silence continued, however, as both the old and young worried about news of a broken dam and floods. Even the choirmaster's composure failed him. Then a clear, calm voice continued the psalm:

> *The voice of the Lord is over the waters,*
> *The God of glory thunders...*

The surprised canons discovered that it was Herman, who was singing with such serenity that one might have thought that it was a sunny, spring day. His composure helped the others recover their wits and continue chanting the psalm:

> *The voice of the Lord is mighty,*
> *The voice of the Lord is majestic.*
> *The voice of the Lord breaks the cedars,*
> *The Lord breaks the cedars of Lebanon.*

"I have come from East Frisia," panted a man disheveled by wind and rain. He told the abbot that he had been riding for ten hours and had seen much devastation. "All the dikes broke in Jeverland, and for miles the sea covers the plains. Farms, houses and entire villages have been destroyed! I heard the death cries of men and

59

animals, but I rode as if I were being chased by a pack of wolves!"

He gasped for breath and wiped his pale, wet forehead. The peasant's trembling hands grasped those of the abbot. "Lord, if our dam breaks too, we are lost. The ice and storm continue to batter it. What shall we do if the dam gives way, Father Abbot?"

"Go to your home," the abbot spoke with calm firmness, as he held the weary man's hands. "Your wife and children are surely worried about you. Go to them. This whole matter rests in God's hands."

"But what shall we do against the flood?" the man sobbed.

"We will build a new dam!" responded the abbot.

"A new dam? *Tonight*?"

"Yes, tonight! We shall build a dam with our prayers! Go home and light a candle before Our Lady. Then pray to Her with your family. That will strengthen the dam that was built with the help of God's grace and is protected by the Blessed Virgin."

The abbot returned to the church as the canons concluded the holy psalm:

*The Lord is enthroned above the flood,*
*The Lord is enthroned as king forever.*
*May the Lord give strength to His people.*
*May the Lord bless His people with peace.*

**\* \* \***

"Blessings on Abbot Frederick," prayed clerics and villagers alike when the storm passed the next day. "A blessing upon the abbot, and blessings on Our Lady and Her dam!" The prayers of the priests and peasants had indeed built the second dam which fortified the first. The storm and ice had caused many weaknesses and breaches in the dam, so Abbot Frederick not only repaired them, but he also built the dam still higher.

The abbot had even loftier expectations for the young men under his care. He often talked to his cloister students, whose youthful vigor and vitality he enjoyed sharing and molding. "The sea is glorious, life is glorious," he told the young men. "Both contain waves of God's unending goodness. But you must be masters of your lives just as the Frisians are masters of the sea. My sons, build dams against the flood. If you do not conquer the roaring flood of life in your early years, then it will rush over you and bring death, not life!"

* * *

Herman built a "holy dam" which he constantly fortified with prayer. He felt the tide of his blood rising as the springtime of youth thundered in his heart. No waves of unruly passion profaned his heart, mind, or body, however, because of the strength he derived from his life of prayer. He often prayed before Our Lady in church, and he always carried her image in his mind and heart. Because Herman was Our Lady's child, he allowed nothing into his life which would diminish her honor. Wherever there are shores, people battle against the sea. More daunting, however, and more important is the war waged by the young man who builds a dam against the sinful passions of his heart.

* * *

Later that spring Abbot Frederick announced to the cloister students news of profound importance: "Once again, the hand of God has been felt guiding His Church. The schism has ended. Victor, the false pope supported by Emperor Frederick Barbarossa, is dead. Pray for his soul, which departed from this life under the sentence of excommunication. Pray also for Pope Alexander, the rightful heir to the throne of Peter. Remember also the emperor and the Holy Roman Empire, that they will channel their earthly power to promote God's will, and not to divide God's Church. And, finally, pray also for our archbishop, Rainald von Dassel, so that, as chancellor of the emperor, God will enlighten him to provide sound counsel and spiritual guidance to our ruler."

Herman recalled two years earlier when the mighty Rainald von Dassel had humbly requested his prayers. He had prayed a great deal for the archbishop ever since. On that day, Herman prayed especially fervently.

* * *

Bad news came to the cloister two years later. Even after Victor's death, Emperor Frederick had continued to defy Pope Alexander. Following the chancellor's bad advice, he colluded with a minority of cardinals to set up Guido of Crema as 'Pope' Paschal III. At the time of the news, the emperor was marching to Rome with a great army to enthrone Paschal.

A tremendous battle between the armies of the true pope and those of the emperor occurred at Tusculum. Victory seemed imminent for the pope's forces when Rainald von Dassel himself seized the banner of Cologne bearing the image of St. Peter. Then he and three hundred German knights savagely charged the papal ranks and caused them great losses. Triumphantly entering the Holy City of Rome with his chancellor, Emperor Frederick solemnly enthroned the false pope in Saint Peter's Basilica. He now enjoyed the pinnacle of earthly power.

"The archbishop sure is brave!" marveled Conrad. "Only a hero could lead the charge as the banner bearer!"

Herman said nothing, but his friend noticed a deep sadness in his eyes. Then he went to the church to pray before the statue of the Queen of Heaven. It was the day before the feast of the Assumption of the Blessed Virgin Mary in the year 1167. Hour after hour Herman remained immersed in deepest prayer for the archbishop. Conrad entered the church once, but he could not bring himself to disturb his friend so lost in his prayer. It grew dark before Herman finally left the church. As the bells announced the coming of the great feastday, Herman walked through the cloister grounds. He glowed with the light of great joy, knowing that Mary had heard her child.

* * *

Rainald von Dassel lay on his deathbed. It was the evening before the feast of the Assumption of the Blessed Virgin Mary. He and twenty-five thousand of the emperor's soldiers had contracted the plague. The chancellor groaned and covered his disfigured face with a pillow.

"O God, You are cruel!"

"God is just!" answered a black-robed monk standing nearby. "You have sinned seriously against Him by dividing His Church. You thought you could build a dam against God, but God has broken your dam like a plaything. Now you feel the flood of God's wrath!"

"God has broken the dam," Rainald struggled to say. "Father, where is the emperor?"

"The emperor has fled."

"The emperor has *fled*? He's left me alone? And where is Paschal?"

"Guido Cardinal of Crema, the false pope, has also fled."

"He, too, has fled?" groaned the archbishop before he let out a ghastly laugh. "All of them have fled. Everything is over. All is lost!"

"You are not abandoned, Rainald von Dassel." The monk's tone grew softer. "God's grace awaits you. Think back on your life, chancellor. Recall some good deeds you performed for the poor, the sick and those in sorrow. Perhaps those hands are folded now in prayer for you. These prayers are powerful with God."

"I was a man of power, not a man of piety, Father. I helped the poor through administrative effectiveness, but I was not a priest of the people." Rainald moaned in pain and despair.

Then a picture suddenly entered his mind. The dying man recalled that the image was from not that long ago, maybe only five years. A child had come to see him about riding a donkey, and the archbishop had asked for his prayers. This thought brought great peace to the sick man.

"You might be right, Father," he whispered almost inaudibly. "There may be one person praying for me...."

"Make your peace with God!" urged the monk.

"Yes, I will make my peace! Peace with God and peace with Alexander, *Pope* Alexander. Come, hear my confession, Father."

The dying man, who had so strongly felt the justice of God, now experienced the healing wonder of Divine Mercy. The priest then freed him from his sins and the penalty of excommunication, and, with the greatest devotion, Archbishop Rainald received the Holy Eucharist and was anointed with the sacrament of Extreme Unction.

Rainald von Dassel heard the monk's words growing dimmer. He saw a distant light coming nearer. Then he recognized the shimmering light to be the robe of Our Lady, who brought peace to the once unhappy man.


Months later, loyal followers of the chancellor brought his body home to Cologne. In the Cathedral Chapel of Our Lady he found his final resting place under an ancient statue of the Blessed Virgin Mary.

## Chapter Eleven
# Life at Mariëngaarde

**B**ecause shepherd's work is steeped in solitude, shepherds are often quiet, reflective people, either by nature or necessity. Ludger, the shepherd of the abbey of Mariëngaarde, was just such a man. He kept mostly to himself and spoke little with others, although his lips moved incessantly. One evening Ludger and his dog Beowulf were sitting before the abbey gate staring out into the growing darkness.

"What are you doing, Ludger?" asked a cheerful, young voice.

The shepherd turned suddenly. "Oh, it's you, Herman," he whispered. His eyes were wide with fright. He grabbed the boy's arm and pointed into the night. "Look! There it is! Coming from the moor!"

"I see nothing, nothing at all," Herman said.

"Look!" the shepherd whispered again, this time with growing urgency. "Don't you see that grayness? It's coming from the earth and covering the ground!"

"So? That's just mist rising from the moor."

"*Mist!?* That's not mist!" The shepherd was almost spitting. "You really think it's nothing more than that?! Perhaps you don't know about the ancient Frisian law which decreed that any woman who lost her honor was to be cast into the moor by the men of her tribe. There she would sink and perish into the quicksand with her shame. Many are buried there, and that 'thing' rising from the ground, that thing you call 'mist' is really something much more: it is the ghosts of the women who have been cast into the moor. On nights such as this, they rise from their mournful graves, sweep over the earth, and weep for their lost honor. Listen! Don't you hear their cries and moans?!"

"That's the wind whistling through the fir trees," Herman remarked.

"The wind. You say that like it was nothing at all. Like it had no life. No! Everything is full of life! It's in the firs, in the pines, blowing over the meadows and the moors. From all sides it surrounds us!"

"You're right, Ludger," Herman explained. "Everything is full of life. Everything is full of life because everything is full of God! That's why life is good, because it is from God."

"God?" The old man reflected. "Yes, God is here. He's also in the church and in the sky somewhere, but the earth is where the spooks and spirits and ghosts of these women wander. The grayness is coming nearer. See how the dog is disturbed? He's going to howl."

"Beowulf's got fleas," laughed Herman. "Ludger, you have a wonderful name. Saint Ludger was a great missionary in Westphalia, but your beliefs are those of a heathen."

"I was baptized as a child!" Ludger protested.

"Yes, but you still cling to ancient pagan fears. You see living things in all of nature, but you see them as spooks and evil spirits. You should see God's presence where you see evil."

"But there are spirits of the night. I have felt them many times. They have slithered into my room and squeezed my heart. They've made me cry out in terror!"

"That's just because you ate too much for dinner that evening. There are no 'spirits of the night,' but there is a 'Morning Star,' the glorious Mother of God. Go to her, Ludger. She will cleanse your heart of its anxiety. She's helped me thousands of times. The superstitions of the heathen are nothing but darkness, Ludger. You believe that evil spirits lurk in the shadows ready to frighten and torment you, but our Church offers us nothing but brightness, the purest light of God reflected in Mary and the saints. The glow of such radiance provides great comfort and peace."

Herman urged Ludger once more to approach his mother Mary in prayer. Then he answered the Compline bell and proceeded to the church. During the *Salve Regina*, Herman prayed that the Mother of Life would shine eternal light upon the dark and doubtful soul of the old shepherd. That night, Ludger prayed the *Hail Mary* before lying down on his straw, and this time the "spirits of the night" did not disturb him.

* * *

Herman retained the exceptional joy which radiated from his entire being, but he also grew more quiet, serious, and reflective. However, he was still very much a comrade to his peers, few of whom discerned the depth of his Christ-centered heart. Herman struggled to perceive all of life swirling around him through the eternal perspective of God.

One day the students were reading a story from Ovid's *Metamorphosis* when Conrad whispered to Herman: "That old Ovid gets on my nerves with his ridiculous stories. I get stomach aches from his tapeworm sentences."

"I don't mind that," Herman whispered back. "But what worth do they have in God's eyes?" He decided to pose this question to Father Fridolin.

"In the eyes of God?" repeated the surprised teacher.

"Yes, in God's eyes!" Herman resolutely confirmed. "I don't know why we read the books of pagan authors in an abbey school. Then, in the afternoon, we find so little time to draw from the riches of the Bible and the Fathers of the Church."

"Herman, I'm surprised. Don't you derive any pleasure from these glorious verses? The abbeys have long been famous for being places of classical learning. If monks had not copied these manuscripts, they would have been lost long ago."

"Didn't they have anything better to do?" Conrad interrupted.

"The Church is broad-minded," the teacher asserted. "The Hebrews took gold and silver vessels on their flight from Egypt. Saint Augustine teaches that we Christians now take 'gold and silver' from the books of the Roman poets. They can be used most effectively in preaching the Gospel. The superstitions, the pagan contents of these poems, can no longer harm us, but their beauty can still delight us. True beauty is always a path to God, so what better way is there to praise Him than with the finest literature and art ever created? And the beauty of classical works can also heighten our appreciation of the God Whom the pagans never knew."

Herman could not refute his teacher, so he sat down. What Father Fridolin had said was true, but Herman's intensely personal love for God caused him to view classical works as frivolous detours from Pure Divinity.

Father Fridolin reported the incident to Abbot Frederick after class. The abbot agreed that Herman indeed was different, but he added, "Perhaps he's right. Too seldom we fix our gaze on the Eternal Beauty. One thing is certain: Herman sees more of it than all of us. Have you ever observed him at prayer?"

"Yes. It seems as if he is no longer on earth."

"He is a child of grace!" the abbot declared in admiration. Father Fridolin felt a bit ambivalent when he left the abbot. He respected his singularly blessed student, but the teacher still chafed over the attack upon his beloved Ovid.

* * *

"You've done a good thing, Herman!" Egbert, a sturdy Frisian, congratulated his classmate during recreation. "Father Fridolin bores us all with his Roman nonsense. He should tell us about the heroes of Frisia. Do you know the story of the brave Frisian women who routed the mighty Danes in a great battle?"

Before Herman could answer, Egbert continued, "The Danes invaded a Frisian village, and they overwhelmed the village men with their strength. But then the Frisian women joined the fight. The women took boiling kettles of soup they were preparing for their families, and threw the scalding contents into the faces of those Danish devils. The invaders fled and never returned. That's far greater heroism than you'll read about in the *Metamorphosis*!"

"We should be learning more about God, not fairy tales!" Herman remarked.

"Herman, are you calling the great 'soup battle' a fairy tale? Just say so," Egbert threatened, "and I'll write the entire story on your back!"

Conrad broke in. "Cool down, Egbert. We don't know if that story is really true or not. But I do know a true Frisian story. Your ancestors at Dokkum murdered Saint Boniface in a sneaky and cowardly way!"

Egbert's face grew red, and it seemed as if his anger momentarily paralyzed him. Then he screamed and threw himself upon Conrad. Others joined in, and soon an all-out brawl raged between the Frisians and the other students. Only Abbot Frederick's arrival and thunderous command to stop ended the fray. Many students were badly bruised, scratched, and bleeding.

"*Quadrivium* students," the abbot shouted, "you have acted like little children!"

"Well, we're not going to let ourselves be called cowards!" Egbert shouted back. "A Frisian is nobody's coward!" These words truly resonated with the abbot who was Frisian himself.

"All of you will have an opportunity to show your strength and courage," the abbot declared. "For the next two weeks you can dig in the moors with the brothers. Your excess energy will be put to good use there."

"At least we get two weeks without Ovid," quipped Conrad.

"My young Frisians are wild," the abbot told the prior. "They are wild and rough and stubborn. But they are the real wood from which to carve true sons of Saint Norbert."

\* \* \*

Herman felt a growing distance between himself and his comrades. The bold Frisians belittled Herman's simple, pious ways. His estrangement from them grew wider when Herman was afflicted with an illness that covered his face with sores. The ridicule and repulsion expressed by his classmates pained Herman worse than his sickness. However, on a feast of the Blessed Mother, he was cured.

"He is too sensitive for this land," the prior told the abbot one day. "He should be made stronger and sturdier."

"If you mean he's too soft, you're wrong, Father Prior," the abbot responded. "Herman sleeps on a board instead of straw. He uses a rock as his pillow. He is very hard on himself, but God has given him a very sensitive heart, and God is forming it to perfection!"

## Chapter Twelve
# The Chalice with Three Roses

Leaning heavily on a cane, Sister Iburga hobbled through the streets of Cologne. She had long since retired as cook of Sankt Mergen, and she had become bent and feeble. However, old age had also made her more meek and humble. Sister Iburga had made her peace with the world, even with Sister Prioress, who had forgiven Iburga for calling her a glutton and a fat hen.

Sister had to stop often to catch her breath as she walked to the Benedictine monastery of Saint Pantaleon. She needed to see the famous goldsmith, Master Frederick, whose workshop was located there. When she entered the shop, she was hit by a blast of heat.

To Sister Iburga, the place seemed like a magic kitchen with its pots and vessels and crucibles all bubbling and steaming. The forge's charcoal fire raged in response to the strong draft of the apprentice's bellows. Master Frederick stood at an anvil working on a piece of soft silver. Sister then saw a work of incredible beauty in the back of the workshop. It looked like a miniature church, and it was made entirely from gold and silver. The roof was decorated with precious jewels.

"That is the reliquary for Saint Maurinus, an abbot and martyr of Cologne. It will be enshrined at Saint Pantaleon's," the master told her.

"It's beautiful!" Sister Iburga could not take her eyes off the magnificent work of art.

"It's the crowning achievement of all my work. The very best I could ever do for the honor of God and the glory of His saints," Frederick said proudly. Then he sighed, "Ah, Sister, but another smith has come whose name is Godfrey. He is making a shrine for Archbishop Heribert. When I learned of the fame of his work, I crossed the Rhine to go to Deutz to the shop of this talented Dutchman. I was not prepared to see such splendid and glorious work. I fell on my knees and tears came to my eyes. I shook the hand of Master Godfrey but did not say a word before I left.

"But still another will have to come, even greater. Archbishop Phillip wishes that a reliquary be made in the cathedral for the shrine of the Three Kings. That will be the greatest one on earth! If only I could make it the way my soul sees it." Master

Frederick grew silent again before he finally asked Sister Iburga the reason for her visit.

"I would like you to make a chalice, Master Frederick. I wish to present it to a priest on his ordination day."

"A chalice, Sister! That is a sacred trust even greater than any reliquary. A chalice is the repository of the Lord's Precious Blood! Would you like to see some designs I've already prepared?"

"No, Master, I don't think I'll find the right one among them. I would like three branches growing from the base of the chalice. Then I want them to intertwine until, at the top, they bloom into three roses. Can you do that?"

"That's an unusual request for so holy a vessel. Don't you think it's a bit too worldly?"

"I don't know," the Sister wavered. "He has loved roses all his life. Hundreds of times I have seen him bring them to the statue of Our Lady. He said they were God's most beautiful creations. 'One can smell the love of God in them,' he used to say. That's why I thought it would be a good idea."

"Please let me make the chalice, Master Frederick!" the journeyman apprentice interrupted. "The Sister is right. A new era is coming when men will realize the gentle yet dramatic beauty of all creation. In nature we find the singular beauty of God! Before too long, the great cathedrals will reflect more of this beauty. Master, please let me forge this chalice."

"Nicholas, you have proven the mastery of your craft. Yes, you have my permission. Sister, you will be pleased."

\* \* \*

Herman had almost completed all of the training which would culminate in his priestly ordination. He had long ago taken the vows of poverty, chastity, and obedience. He had thought of the three crowns on the coat of arms of Cologne when he made this sacred, threefold pledge.

The final retreat in preparation for ordination was led by Abbot Werner, Ulrick's successor. As Nicholas forged the gold and silver for the chalice, the abbot formed the hearts of the young men called by God, not only by his words but also by his example.

"Have profound reverence for every heart! God has made each one in the image of the Holy Spirit. Everyone carries this divine image in his heart, and one's task is to become more like this image.

The priestly vocation is to help a man recognize this hidden image and then to help shape his heart into that image. We are like goldsmiths who are forging men's hearts into the glorious image of God! Above all, however, we priests must form our own hearts according to the will of God. Our hearts must become chalices forged in the fire of work, struggle, and sorrow. Abundant earthly pain will produce abundant divine beauty in our souls."

\* \* \*

As Herman advanced, his yearning for solitude increased. He often left his companions to go to the cloister church. There everything worldly disappeared when he knelt before the altar. The endless stream of divine love once again flooded his heart, as it had on the day of his First Holy Communion.

Then Herman discovered the world of mystical prayer. God drew his heart into that sublime light where Eternal Love dwells. This was a place beyond discursive prayer and formal expressions of words. Herman knelt, immersed in awe and wonder, gazing into the light of divinity. The wonder of God's glory overflowed continuously within his soul.

God chooses certain people whom He permits to glance at the normally inaccessible light of His majesty. Especially when humanity is sinful and indifferent, God shows Himself in solitude to the pure of heart. Herman received just such a grace at Steinfeld. His soul was the chalice of purest gold into which God poured out His Fullness. An intense pain pierced Herman's heart during such times, but in its glow, he constantly saw the face of Our Lady who brought him great comfort and peace.

\* \* \*

Bad news came from the south in the spring of 1176. Frederick Barbarossa had once again crossed the Alps with a mighty army. He had attempted to punish the cities of Lombardy, particularly Alessandria, named after Pope Alexander. The emperor's men called it the "straw city" because its first homes had been quickly constructed with roofs of straw. However, the city held out under seven months of siege, during which the ranks of the imperial army were diminished once again by a terrible epidemic.

Henry the Lion, a powerful vassal of the emperor, at length grew disgusted with the protraction of the Italian campaign.

Frederick's army had lost half its members when Henry ordered his men home. The depleted army suffered a terrible defeat at Legnano. Fighting on the front lines, the emperor suffered what appeared to be a fatal spear wound. Many had seen the spear pierce the leader's silver armor, knocking him from his horse.

The emperor's fall demoralized his men, and they made a frenzied retreat leaving immense spoils for the victorious Lombards. Frederick's wife was staying in Pavia, where she remained in mourning. Some weeks later, however, Frederick came and stood before her, alive and well. But his face wore a grave expression, the likes of which she had never seen.

* * *

About that same time the archbishop of Cologne was laying his hands on the head of the Norbertine frater Herman, ordaining him to the holy priesthood. When the *Litany of the Saints* was sung the young priest felt as though earth and heaven had been united in a divine outpouring of love. As the bishop's hands rested upon Herman's head, he felt the hand of God pressing upon his head a crown of all graces.

"Let it be a crown of thorns," Herman prayed. "Lord, bless me with crosses. I wish to be nothing but Your consecrated chalice of suffering. Lord, let me be your sacrifice!"

Herman had often thought about what he should ask God for on his ordination day. He had considered the needs of his cloister; those of his confreres in Steinfeld, Frisia, Bohemia, and Moravia; his mother kneeling nearby; his father, who had died the previous year; the many sorrowful people he saw daily at the cloister gate; and the needs of his own heart.

Yet Herman recognized an even greater need which cried out for help. He thought of the continuing war between the Holy Roman Empire and the Roman Catholic Church. He felt the immense misery caused by the conflict between the emperor and the pope. He saw the harm done to so many souls caused by the schism. It seemed that the troubles of the entire world cried out for Herman's help.

"Priest of God, your arms seize heaven itself. Pray to God that He might put an end to this trouble."

The new priest joined his hands in prayer, and his lips uttered the single request of his ordination: "Lord, give us peace! Mercifully grant peace in our day. End this agony which oppresses our hearts. Grant peace between the Kingdom of God and the Holy Roman Empire."

For the first time, the young priests spoke the prayers of the Mass. In hushed tones they recited the holy text, but at the *Agnus Dei*, the supplication for peace spilled so painfully from Herman's lips that his confreres, and even the bishop, turned to him in astonishment.

"Lamb of God, Who takest away the sins of the world, *grant us peace.*"

**\* \* \***

After the holy ceremony in the cathedral, Herman returned to his home on Stephan Street. Herman's mother overwhelmed him with her love, as she endlessly and respectfully caressed his consecrated hands. That morning she had given her son to God, and her heart was overflowing with joy and gratitude as she recalled the stormy night of her son's birth.

"Now you will be alone, Mother," Herman said as he stroked her snow-white hair.

"The mother of a priest is never alone," she responded. "She is always with her son, and through him, with God."

"Your mother will find a home in the convent of Sankt Mergen," Sister Iburga assured Herman.

"But I am not of the nobility," objected Frau Maria.

"The mother of a priest is the noblest woman in the world," replied the wise nun.

"Herman, I have made a corporal for you," his mother said after a pause. "My hands shake so much, and my eyes are no longer so good. A few stitches are surely out of line. But if it isn't too badly made, if you would place the Body of Christ on it, I would be so happy!"

"Oh, Mother," Herman answered, "it will be my most precious corporal. I will use it only on the highest feasts of the Church: Easter, Christmas, Pentecost, and on all the feasts of Our Lady." Herman kissed his mother's trembling hands.

"Herman," his mother continued, "my name is Maria, and when you place the Holy Eucharist on this corporal, then I shall feel like the Blessed Virgin herself, who placed the linens on the crib of Jesus. You mustn't laugh at this. Perhaps I am just old and getting a little senile."

"No! You're right, Mother!" Herman exclaimed.

"You know we are far from being rich, Herman, but Sister Iburga has brought you something that will surely surprise you."

Sister's trembling hands opened a finely-carved case, revealing a golden chalice framed in velvet. Herman gasped as he laid his eyes upon it.

"This is for your First Mass," the old nun said. "The bishop has already consecrated it."

"This… is… *my* chalice?" Herman stammered. He removed the chalice from its case and held it up to the sunlight. Then he looked at Sister Iburga with eyes of deep appreciation.

"I wanted another pillow for my golden throne in heaven," she joked.

"There are roses on the chalice! How beautiful!"

"I knew how much you liked roses. A journeyman named Nicholas from Lorraine made it. He hated to part with it once he had finished it. He even visited Sankt Mergen to see it one last time."

"This is the work of no journeyman. This is the creation of a master." Herman caressed the three golden roses. "I cannot adequately express my thanks right now. I will do so tomorrow when I elevate this chalice at the Holy Sacrifice."

\* \* \*

Master Martin, the shoemaker from Malzbuchel, arrived later to congratulate Herman. Since the others were too overjoyed to talk much, Martin once again told the story of the Cologne Crusade, the storming of Lisbon, and the miracle of Saint Ursula and the eleven thousand Virgins. Then he informed Herman that Margaret had entered the Norbertine convent in Fussenich.

"She wants to know if you ever think of Saint Joseph and his pretzels. She also asked if you are now going to show the Savior and Our Lady to the entire world. I think my little girl is losing her right mind under that holy veil."

"No, she's sane enough," smiled Herman. "Write to her and tell her that I understand her message perfectly."

When Herman inquired about his former companions back home, Martin knew all the news. Stephen had joined a large trading company and was becoming very wealthy. Herman asked about Peter, and the shoemaker scratched his head.

"After you left he became a wild boy indeed. His hot temper and dishonest ways caused him all sorts of problems. Right now he's in the emperor's army in Italy, but no one has heard from him."

Herman thought a long time about the restless boy who accompanied him throughout the crypts of the Cologne churches, seeking true greatness and nobility.

Later that evening, Herman climbed the stairs to his attic bedroom. He held a candle in one hand and the chalice in the other; he could not part from it. Entering his old room, he found white roses strewn everywhere. The room was filled with their fragrance.

"A greeting from Mary! A gift from Our Lady!" Herman shouted. Then he filled the cup of his new chalice with the miraculous flowers.

\* \* \*

The next morning, Herman covered Mary's altar with the white roses before he celebrated his First Holy Mass. When he elevated the chalice at the consecration, a stream of sunshine bathed its flowers in a dazzling light.

In the shadow of a pillar, the journeyman Nicholas gazed with burning eyes at the chalice containing the Precious Blood. Above the hands of the young priest, Nicholas saw the golden roses gleaming in the sunlight and thought to himself, "My creation has now achieved its glorification."

Near the altar an old woman bowed her head in deep prayer: the mother of the newly ordained priest stood near the first sacrifice of her son, just as the Mother of God stood near the Cross. Frau Maria offered her own sacrifice to Christ crucified.

What the soul of the young priest felt at that moment, no pen could ever capture or record.

## Chapter Thirteen
# Holy Service, Penance, and the Miracle of Peace

**F**ather Herman and Father Arnulf are assigned to table duty," announced Abbot Werner at the Steinfeld cloister's first meeting with the newly ordained priests.

"The lean and fat years," whispered Father Albert jokingly to his neighbor, Father Anthony. "They remind me of my namesake," replied Father Anthony. "When they serve at the table, Herman will look like Saint Anthony, the austere hermit, standing next to his well fed pig!"

"Such ideas you have!" whispered Albert with mock indignation. "How can you speak so uncharitably about our corpulent confrere?"

"Oh, the comparison is only in the fat...."

"Father Anthony will assist Father Erwin with the copying of the Bible," proclaimed the abbot. "There he will learn to control his loose tongue because dear Father Erwin is, unfortunately, stone deaf."

Now it was Father Albert who grinned mischievously at his neighbor.

"Tomorrow, Father Conrad will travel to Mariengarten. There he will lead some Frisian settlers to Bohemia where he will receive further instructions."

"*Fiat, fiat*," stammered the chosen priest. His secret longing had always been to go east as a pioneer for God and empire. Canons and settlers who worked this new land established a wall of Christianity against the menace of the Mongols and Tartars. One plowed the fields and chopped wood while armed with a sword in this land. Many had perished in the wild, harsh region, but travel to the east was the greatest honor for a Premonstratensian. At the end of the meeting, the chapter congratulated Father Conrad, the chosen one.

"You will miss our homeland very much, Conrad," said Herman as he offered his hand to his friend.

"Yes, but that is nothing compared to the opportunity of tilling new land for God's empire. Besides, I am always at home in the habit of Saint Norbert. Of course, I will often think of you serving the tables with fat Arnulf!" The jolly canon could not resist one last joke.

Arnulf arrived presently, rubbing his thick hands in anticipation. "Herman, we've been assigned a fine post. It's good to be connected to the kitchen!"

"I doubt the smells from the kitchen will satisfy my spiritual hunger," Herman responded reluctantly.

"You can always enter the hermitage in Duvenforest."

"Arnulf, you are neither wise nor noble when you mock things you do not understand," Herman retorted. "Hermits are earnest, magnanimous people. They realize humanity's need for prayer and penance, especially during these sinful and violent times. They surrender their freedom in order to promote God's reign of blessings. I feel only admiration for these 'prisoners for Christ.'"

"A mother who raises her children for Christ deserves more honor than pious hermits," Conrad asserted.

"You may be right," conceded Herman. "Motherhood is a very great honor. But it doesn't diminish the work of repentance, especially when it's performed happily before God."

"I will not contradict you, my friend," concluded Conrad.

"Someone's salvation may come from a cloister or hermitage which he had never even heard of. I believe world history can be changed by those who humbly serve God in silence and anonymity," Herman continued. "We are ultimately not under the power of rulers, but in the hands of God. Prayers and sacrifices move God to dispense His blessings."

"You're right, Herman." Conrad looked directly into his friend's eyes. "And because of that, I have one request before I leave: please pray for me, Herman!"

"I will never forget you," Herman assured him, moved by his friend's request.

"I will be forever indebted to you. You also owe me a large debt for the 'baptism' I gave you in the wash basin." Both friends departed in laughter.


Later that week, the two new priests served at table for the first time. No one could suppress a smile as the canons, one slender and one stout, appeared with their bowls. Arnulf rested two bowls on his ample belly. Even the abbot could barely contain his laughter, and the reader lost his place in the *Life of Saint Norbert* on account of the distraction.

✳ ✳ ✳

Table service at the cloister of Steinfeld was a lot of work. While Father Arnulf enjoyed the advantages of kitchen work, Herman was saddened by the loss of precious time for prayer and meditation. The two servers usually had to leave religious services early in order to prepare the tables.

One aspect of the job delighted Herman however: because the servers ate their meal only after everyone else had finished, Herman could fast for many days without being noticed. Fasting was easily noticed at the community table. Now Father Arnulf was the only one who knew about it, and he was quite happy to receive Herman's portions.

Herman worked as a table server for an entire year before he decided to ask the abbot to relieve him of this duty. He went first to the church to ask Mary for advice. Herman prayed more fervently than he had in a long time, and a deep melancholy overwhelmed his soul.

"Holy Mother, you know my heart's desire. I wish only to love you and your Son. I beg you: please take from me this job, which distracts me from your presence and burdens me with worldly concerns."

Our Lady's answer entered Herman's soul with absolute clarity: "Know that you have no greater duty than to serve your brothers in charity."

Herman left the church feeling wonderfully consoled. Now he saw the importance and dignity of his work. He returned to his cell where he found his Bible lying open. The abbot, aware of the young priest's struggle, had opened the Bible to the thirty-second chapter of Saint Luke's Gospel: "...the greatest among you must act as if he were the least, the leader as if he were the one who serves. For who is greater, the one at table or the one who serves? The one at table, surely? Yet here am I among you as One Who serves!"

Herman closed the Bible and prayed with all his heart, "Thank You, Lord, for the office You have given me."

✳ ✳ ✳

A short time later, however, the abbot did transfer Herman from his work in the refectory to the sacristy of the abbey church. After serving at the canons' table, he was now to serve at God's table. Herman eagerly entered his new position. He prepared the altar, chalice and vestments with profound reverence. His greatest joy, though, was that his service kept him near the tabernacle. His prayer and work shone more brightly with the glow of the sanctuary lamp.

Herman knelt for long hours before the doors of the tabernacle behind which dwelt the Lord. His lips continued to utter the prayer of his ordination day: "Lord, let there be peace!" The division between Church and empire had continued to tear at the young priest's heart.

During harvest time, nearly all the community worked in the fields, but Herman remained in work and prayer around the sanctuary. The sharpening of sickles could be heard in the stillness of the church.

"Lord, grant peace," cried the heart of the canon, "peace to the Church, peace to the Holy Roman Empire! Heavenly Mother, intercede for us. Strike my heart with a thousand torments, but give us peace!"

\* \* \*

Father Anthony suddenly entered the church and, with hurried steps, approached the young priest immersed in prayer. "Herman, you must ring the bells! There is peace! The emperor has made peace with Pope Alexander. There is peace!"

Herman threw open the church doors and, seeing a few cloister students, enlisted them to help him ring the bells. Rejoicing students stormed the ropes and soon all the bells of Steinfeld rang out over the Eifel. Father Herman himself rang the large bell of Mary with tearful eyes and a joyful heart and with every ring of the bell his heart cried out, "Peace, peace!"

The news of peace even reached the settlers traveling to Bohemia. They, too, were jubilant. When Conrad heard the news, he remembered Herman's words remarking that world history could be changed by those who serve God in silence and humility, the unknown and hidden ones. "You are right, old friend," Conrad said to himself. "The peace of Venice is truly a miracle of grace." And back in the cloister at Steinfeld Herman continued until evening time ringing the bell of Our Lady: "Peace! Peace! There is Peace!"

# Photographic Section:

*(For more detailed information regarding the artwork depicted on these pages, please see pages 6 & 7 of the introduction).*

*p. 80: Stained glass detail.*
*p. 81: Stained glass window in St. Michael's Abbey Church: St. Herman Joseph holding the Christ Child.*
*pp. 82-83: Stained glass window in the sacristy of St. Michael's Abbey: St. Herman Joseph gathering pure water for Mass (all stained glass is by John Bera Studios).*
*pp. 84-87: Scenes from the Cactus garden at St. Michael's with St. Herman Joseph writing his hymn to the Sacred Heart of Jesus (by Bill Conger).*
*pp. 88-89: Statue of St. Herman Joseph in the Sacristy of St. Michael's Abbey Church.*
*pp. 90-91: Wood carving in the dormitory of St. Michael's Prep.*
*p. 92: Painting of St. Herman Joseph giving the apple to Jesus in the Mindszenty Chapel at St. Michael's.*
*p. 93: Painting of St. Herman Joseph writing his hymn to the Sacred Heart of Jesus in the Mindszenty Chapel at St. Michael's.*
*p. 94: Painting of St. Michael in St. Michael's Abbey church.*
*p. 95: Painting of St. Norbert in St. Michael's Abbey church (the painting series is by Wolfgang Köberl).*

*All photos of stained glass by Richard Belcher*

81

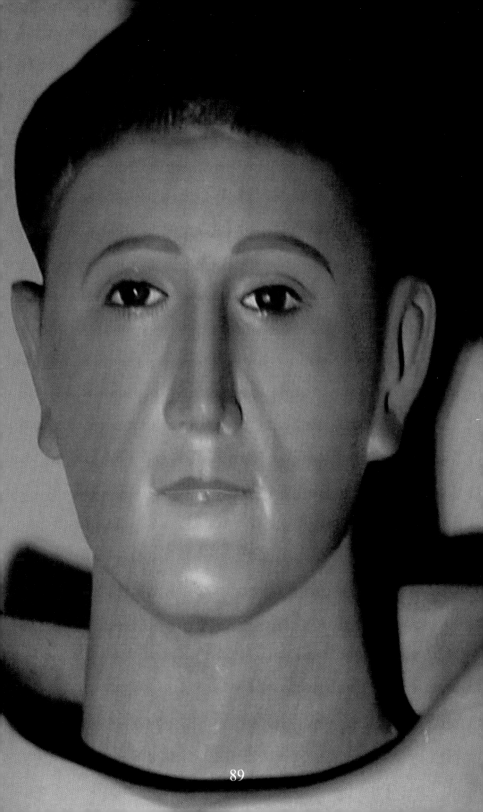

90

W.KÖBERL
1977

AD
OMNE
BONUM
OPUS
PARATI

## Chapter Fourteen
# The Lord over Twenty Nations and the Head Bandit

Old Andrew sat by the hearth and threw a beechwood log into the crackling fire. His wrinkled, smiling face glowed with happiness bathed in the reflection of the flames. He laughed as he turned to Herman who sat next to him.

"Everything is fine with me, Father. I'm not poor. I've already come through the winter without having to stand in the soup line at the monastery. In fact, you think you're speaking with an old peasant, but I'm actually above Emperor Frederick. You see, the emperor rules over Germany and Italy, but I rule over twenty nations. I have hundreds of thousands of subjects, and many queens stand in my service."

"You're speaking of your bees, of course," laughed Herman.

"Yes, my bees. They are good little creatures, so diligent and brave."

"But sometimes they sting!"

"Yes they do, but it feels like a caress to an old beekeeper like me. The human sting is more poisonous and causes more grief. So, Father Herman, have you come for some wax?"

"Yes, please. Twice as much as last time."

"Never have so many candles burned at Steinfeld monastery! But that means you are a good sacristan, Herman. Everyone needs good candle wax these days when suspicious bands of men lurk in the Eifel forests. The Evil One practices his game there, Father Herman." The beekeeper hastily made the sign of the Cross.

"The Evil One has no power over men with good hearts," the priest remarked.

"You are a good man, Father, but you don't know much about the devil. Listen, and I will tell you the story of Duvenstein:

"Over two hundred years ago, the devil possessed the body of a handsome, young knight named Fariant, a member of the court of Count Siegbold of Uhr. Siegbold was a jolly fellow who loved hunting and hawking. Fariant believed that, with a little diabolical magic, he could trap Siegbold in his clutches.

"Count Siegbold must have smelled the sulfurous vapors, though, for he devised a plan to drive away his dangerous companion. Fariant cheerfully agreed to help Siegbold build a hunting lodge in the Eifel Forest. He even hauled the heaviest stones himself. Halls and towers were rapidly constructed, but Fariant roared a thunderous curse when he saw what the crafty count had erected on one of the towers.

"When Fariant questioned the count in a fiery rage, Siegbold asked with a smile, 'Have you ever seen a monastery without a cross?' When the devil knew he'd been fooled, he furiously flung a tremendous stone across the land. That is the story of Duvenstein and the foundation of the monastery at Steinfeld."

"That's just an old wives' tale, although it is entertaining," Herman said with a smile.

"An old wives' tale?! All the old folks in the Eifel will tell you the same story. The devil sweeps through the moors and forest, and he lurks along the walks and in the towers of Steinfeld. Believe me, the Evil One wanders through Duvenstein. Last night I saw fires between the trees, the devil's lights! That's why it's good to light so many candles in the church!"

"Andrew, you love to speak of ghosts. Still you are right. Where the lights of God burn, the devil has no entrance."

Father Herman trudged back to the monastery, immersed in thought as he carried his load of wax. An icy wind blew over the moors and fields, which were blanketed in snow. Passing through Duvenforest, Herman spied some obscure figures moving through the trees. He told himself it was probably just some men gathering wood, and he returned to the beauty of the snowy scene bathed in the glow of dusk and the rising moon.

*Ice and snow, praise the Lord!*
*Dew and frost, praise the Lord!*

Herman clasped the wax in his hands as he prayed the *Canticle of the Three Youths*. He reflected on the simple beauty of the wax with its breath of the moors and sweet scent of honey. He would soon transform it into a resplendent offering which would burn on the altar in the abbey church.

\* \* \*

"Herman, watch carefully tonight!" warned Egbert, the Frisian confrere, when the sacristan returned later that evening. It was Herman's turn to watch over the monastery until the midnight Office. "Suspicious characters have been sighted in this area. I know you heard the dogs howling last night. And did you hear about Himmerod? Thieves broke into the sacristy and stole several

97

chalices. Maybe I should watch with you, Herman."

"No, Egbert, you need your rest. I'll be fine. Thank you for your offer, though."

"You're welcome. Good night, Herman. And good luck."

Herman heard Egbert's footsteps echo down the corridor. A door closed in the distance. Then all became as still as midnight, though the time was barely past eight. The hours before Matins were the time of Herman's most devout prayer. Enveloped in silence and darkness, Herman felt the peace of God's proximity. Only the sanctuary lamp glowed before the tabernacle, and one candle burned before the statue of Mary. The deep stillness was filled with the peace of God and Our Lady.

Herman knelt before the tabernacle, as usual, but tonight he could not suppress a certain uneasiness. He became distracted by the crackle of a candle, the creak of a panel, or the breath of a breeze. He finally got up, walked to the sacristy, lit a lantern there, and then paced through the monastery halls. The security of the monastery was in his hands.

He eventually returned to the sacristy to mold some candles. This work usually engrossed him, causing the hours to fly by quickly. But not tonight. Herman kept glancing at the clock, whose single hand showed the time passing all too slowly. He now regretted rejecting Egbert's offer to watch with him.

\* \* \*

Nearby in Duvenforest, three shabby figures crouched by a fire staring silently into the flames. One of the men wore a leather eye patch. He broke the silence by cursing his comrade who was dressed in an old soldier's uniform.

"By the devil, Captain, I don't know you any more! You used to be the daredevil among us. The instigator. The leader. Now you hang your head like you've got a rope around it."

The man he addressed continued to stare into the fire. The third figure, the one with a severely pock-marked face, offered the captain a jug of wine. He brusquely refused it. Offended by this, the third vagabond joined his comrade in upbraiding their leader. "Remember who led us against the Cistercians in Himmerod? How can you forget our glorious plunder? The Steinfeld monastery is just as rich. Chalices, monstrances, and all that other sacred nonsense that better serves us melted down. You've gotta lead us again, Captain, if you want to keep your share."

"Both of you be quiet!" The captain's eyes burned more fiercely than the fire. Still, he said nothing to them. Instead, he wandered off alone into the snow-covered forest.

"It's that priest, I tell you," whispered the man with the eye patch. "Ever since he saw that priest in the forest he's lost control. But give him a little time. He'll be the same old captain again."

The captain cursed himself. He couldn't blame his cohorts for their surprise. They'd never seen him act this way. He just could not erase the sight of the face of that priest. It was the eyes. No one else had eyes like those of his childhood friend. What nonsense! he told himself. Herman couldn't have been there in the forest. He's in Frisia or Bohemia or somewhere else. Why miss out on Steinfeld's treasures because of some fantasy?

He returned to the fire and demanded the jug of wine. After a long drink, he made an announcement: "Off to Steinfeld! There's gold to be had! Hurry up, before that Matins bell wakes up the whole monastery!"

* * *

"Praise God, only one more hour until Matins!" Herman said as he returned to his candle-making. Suddenly he jumped up. He heard a noise in the chapel. Or was it the cloister? He walked with a shaking lantern through the cloister and then to the chapel. There was a strange patch of light by the Madonna. Herman approached and lifted up his lantern to Mary's crown of stars. Then he fell back. The Holy Virgin now stood before him. This was no representation, but the living Queen of Heaven herself.

"Why is your heart so restless tonight? Why have you no words of prayer in your heart?" The Madonna's words came from an ever-brightening light.

"I must watch, Holy Mother. The times are bad!"

"Watch and pray!" answered the voice from the light.

"The security of the cloister is my responsibility!"

"In my hands rests the monastery of Steinfeld!" came the heavenly response.

"In your hands, Blessed Mother. Yes, in your hands," stammered the priest with joy. Then he fell on his knees and prayed with all his might before Mary's statue.

\* \* \*

A long time passed before some subtle but unmistakable noises distracted Herman once again. He heard the sound of metal being twisted and bent. Someone was trying to break through the monastery gate!

"Can't you go any faster?" the captain whispered urgently. "We must finish before the pious company comes down to pray."

Just then, the door of the cloister directly in front of the gate opened, and someone approached the gate holding a lantern. His breath billowed in the cold, but his voice sounded unusually calm. "Why are you disturbing our peaceful cloister?" The three figures jumped back with shock as the priest opened the gate.

Then the pockmarked man regained his senses and raised his heavy club with an ominous intention. Before he could wield it, however, he was struck to the ground. He looked up to see the captain standing between him and the priest.

"Anyone who touches this priest will pay with his life!" the captain said.

Then the captain grabbed a torch and held it up close to the priest's face. The familiar sound of the canon's voice was confirmed by the unmistakable brilliance of his eyes.

"Herman! Herman!" groaned the bandit incredulously.

"Why have you come to Steinfeld, Peter?" Herman calmly asked.

"I don't know."

"But I do know, Peter," came the gentle response. "You are seeking God's grace. You are seeking the Madonna who has sought you for so long."

The bandit cried out and ran off into the darkness. His two cohorts, who were totally confused and amazed by what had just transpired, soon followed him. By this time other confreres had risen, grabbed weapons, and rushed to the entrance. Herman was just shutting the gate. He turned with a smile and said, "Go to the church. Nothing is the matter here, just a lost traveler knocking at the gate."

Herman then went to the tower and rang the Matins bell. It sang a song of the peace of the Mother of God. For the fleeing bandit, however, each peal struck like the crack of a whip. Herman sensed this, and so he knelt before the statue of the Blessed Virgin in prayer for his childhood friend Peter until dawn.

## Chapter Fifteen
# The Journey of the Three Kings from the West

The rattling of the huge keys silenced the knocking outside Cologne's massive cathedral door. With great effort, the sacristan opened it to the cold of the night and to a pale, serious face with steaming breath illuminated by a thick candle.

The sacristan knew this routine. Regularly, yet not predictably, this familiar late-night visitor appeared at the cathedral door requesting some time for prayer: "The day belongs to my work, but an hour of the night belongs to God," the visitor would say.

"That's all right," replied the sacristan, refusing the coin thrust into his palm. "I'll return in an hour to close up."

Solitary steps echoed throughout the church until the man knelt before an image of the Madonna. He placed his candle in a holder and looked up at Mary. Then he hid his face in his hands and remained frozen in prayer.

After a long time, he raised his head and emitted a long and painful groan. Then he lamented loudly in the darkness: "Lord, I have reached my limit! This job is too big for me. It is crushing me! Lord, you Yourself must guide my hand and my hammer if you want this work to be accomplished!" His last word echoed throughout the church's high vaults.

"To You will go all the honor and the glory. But You will not be honored if I cannot finish, Lord. You must guide my disabled hand, and You must also dissolve the darkness in my soul. For the sake of Your Church, Lord, and for the honor of the Three Holy Kings who rest in this tomb, please give me the inspiration and strength to finish this work."

The man fell silent once more, but his soul continued his plea. Then the glow of his fervor sparked the light of inspiration, and the work of the Holy Spirit was wrought before him in a most beautiful vision. The artist cried out at the brilliance of the image within his soul: the shrine of the Three Kings.

The vision gradually faded, but its imprint was marked indelibly on the soul of the man in prayer. He suddenly felt more peaceful, yet also invigorated with energy. He could not wait to return to his workshop. Then he felt a hand on his shoulder. He turned to see a man wearing a tormented expression and tattered clothing.

"Pardon me. I found the church open and heard you praying. Say, aren't you Master Nicholas of Lorraine, the man working on the shrine of the Three Kings?"

"How do you know me?"

"I have seen your workshop many times, although I looked with bad intentions, to be sure. You own much gold and silver, and I have also seen many gems."

"You're a thief!" whispered Nicholas.

"Red Peter is my name. You may have heard of me." He noticed the artist's violent quivers. "But don't worry; that's all in the past. I am an outcast from all my companions now, both good and evil."

"What do you want from me?"

"Sir, you are a goldsmith, an artist. You can blend gold and silver, but could you also mend a torn and broken heart?"

"Come with me," said Nicholas, and the two men left the church. They walked silently through the dark streets of Cologne until Nicholas stopped at a house. He unlocked a few doors and led Peter into a room where he lit many candles. "This is my workshop," he said.

Peter gasped when he saw the half-finished treasure of the Three Kings' shrine.

"It will be glorious beyond all measure," Nicholas said, "but it is God's work, not mine. Yet I know another shrine much more beautiful and more valuable. It makes this shrine seem pitiful."

"Impossible! What shrine is that?" asked Peter.

"Your soul. Peter, you asked me if my hand could cure your heart. My art does not reach that far. But I do know someone who understands how: a priest in a cloister. He will help you reassemble the shattered shrine of your soul."

"Who is he? Where does he live?"

"It is Father Herman of the Premonstratensian cloister of Steinfeld."

"No, not him! I can't even look him in the eyes. Not before I've done penance."

"You're right, Peter. Repentance will heal your torn heart and give it peace."

"How can I do penance?" Peter asked.

Nicholas appeared deep in thought as he walked around the shrine. Then he said: "The three most powerful kings on earth are now marching toward the Holy Land: Frederick, Emperor of the Germans, Richard the Lionheart from England, and Philip Augustus of France. They are going there in the name of Jesus Christ. Do penance by following the cross. That will give you peace."

Nicholas knew from Peter's joyful response that his words had indeed convinced the troubled young soul. He smiled as the young man rushed off into the night.

* * *

Horrible reports had recently come from the Holy Land. Sultan Saladin had stormed Jerusalem, where he defeated the Christian army and executed countless numbers of its knights. Then he further desecrated the holy city by converting its churches into stables and destroying its crucifixes and bells. This news served to inspire concern and righteous anger in many throughout Europe and led to the launching of a new Crusade.

In the spring of 1189, the Crusaders started off for Jerusalem. "Christ rules! Christ conquers!" became the battle cry for fifteen hundred Cologne Crusaders whose banners of Saint Peter and the Three Kings flew high before them. Among the soldiers marching behind Emperor Frederick Barbarossa was Herman's childhood friend, "Red Peter."

Father Egbert was also in the ranks, serving as a field chaplain. "May God have mercy on the Turkish skulls," laughed the hearty Frisian, wielding his club as he departed from Steinfeld. Several of the brothers and older students had joined him.

The younger boys could not go on the Crusade, so they satisfied themselves with games between Christians and Turks. The brave men who did join the holy endeavor were supported by the confreres remaining at the abbey by their prayers and penance. Even the corpulent Father Arnulf, who at first appeared reluctant, fasted once a week for the intention of the success of the Crusade.

Herman rang the bell of Our Blessed Lady for thirty minutes every day. His prayers increased in fervor and his acts of mortification became even more intense. He implored God to let him share in the pain of the Crusaders whom he was unable to join. Herman suffered a painful gastric ailment which seemed to consume him with fire and which allowed him little sleep. Even in his

103

weakened state, he maintained his prayerful vigils. When his confreres advised him to moderate his austerity, Herman responded, "We can sleep when the Crusade is over. Now we must watch, we must pray, and we must suffer."

\* \* \*

The priest continued to kneel before the tabernacle begging God to send him more suffering, and God sent him a scourge more powerful than any physical ailment. God sent him spiritual suffering. Herman experienced no consolation in prayer. He who had enjoyed the very Light of God was now cast into deepest darkness. Herman continued to kneel before the tabernacle, but the lonely sufferer's soul cried out with the torment of Golgotha: "My God, my God, why have You forsaken me?"

Herman was quite disturbed for many weeks. His confreres did not recognize their brother who was once so serene. Those who tried to speak with him did so in vain: "What can men say if God no longer speaks?" he would ask. Herman found no comfort in prayer, no power in the sacraments. He approached the altar with fear and misgiving. Feastdays, which had once caused him so much rejoicing, now tormented him. God had thrown his heart into the abyss of lamentations, and the entire cloister community pitied Herman. Yet no one spoke with him, for they did not want to increase his sorrow.

On Christmas Eve, Herman suffered greater pain than ever before. He was not even able to perform his duties as sacristan, and his place in the choir at Matins remained empty. Many of the priests could not hide their sadness as they began to pray the Christmas psalms.

However, when the midnight bell rang, God provided instant relief to Herman's troubled soul. Herman experienced an unspeakable consolation. The love of God and the goodness of the Virgin Mary filled the void in his empty and arid soul. He rushed to the church and rejoiced in the glow of its brightness, and his joy was reflected in the faces of his confreres. Then he joined the chanting of the psalms with a strong voice.

In the sacristy after Mass on Christmas Day, Herman noticed that the clock's weights had fallen out of position. He carefully put them back into place. Then he turned to one of his confreres and said,

"The heart is like a clock. Grief is the weight which the heart needs to maintain its peace. But when the suffering becomes too great, it oppresses the heart, and, like the clock, it will not run any more. Then God pushes the weight of the heart back to its correct position."

* * *

That same morning, Master Nicholas entered his workshop to admire his creation in honor of the Three Kings, while the German Crusaders celebrated Christmas Mass outside the gates of Constantinople. Emperor Frederick's eyes gleamed with victory, and Peter's burned with the longing for greater penance. Within the furnace of God's love, these two seemingly unrelated events became fitted together like the parts of a clock.

## Chapter Sixteen
# The Miracle of Our Lady

The prioress of the convent at Fussenich made sure no one was in the sacristy before she approached its clock. Certain that she was unobserved, she shifted the weights and yanked on the chain until the links slipped off the cogs of the wheels. Thanks be to God, it stopped, she said to herself before yelling out the window into the courtyard, "Sister Margaret!"

A cheerful response preceded the youthful Sister's entry. She looked at her superior and then at the clock to which she was pointing. Sister Margaret was both familiar and pleased with Prioress Jepa's broken clock routine.

"It is quite still, Mother Prioress. What shall we do about it?" she asked, quelling the urge to smile at this bit of mischief.

"We will have to send again for Father Herman from Steinfeld. Only he knows how to fix our clock."

"Yes, Father Joseph can do anything," Sister Margaret agreed.

"You mean 'Father *Herman*,' Sister." Margaret sheepishly nodded before the prioress continued, "Tell Alderic to hitch up the horse and go get Father Herman. And tell him to hurry. How can we maintain our schedule without this clock?"

"Father can also give us some spiritual guidance. I'll tell Alderic to ask Father to prepare some points for reflection."

The swinekeeper, Alderic, had also become familiar with this routine, but he remained mystified by it. He could not understand why the clock was breaking so often. It had been accurate and reliable for so long. "The problems didn't start until Father Herman began coming here," he said to his old gray horse when they were a safe distance from the convent.

Father Herman had earned a reputation for his excellent repair of broken timepieces. However, the convents in Fussenich and Meer sought him so often because Father Herman understood hearts as well as clocks. Even pious nuns such as Sister Jepa needed consolation, and Father Herman's mere presence had a healing effect. He himself was a man afflicted with pain, and his words touched their souls like no one else's. Herman's suffering had fashioned within him both profound wisdom and genuine kindness.

The swinekeeper rode through the Eifel toward Steinfeld. A humble and quiet man, he had come to Fussenich a few years earlier and was employed tending the pigs. The pigs were quite satisfied with him.

Urging the old horse on, Alderic reflected on the many tragedies which had occurred since his arrival. Frederick Barbarossa had drowned in a river in a distant land, leaving the German Empire without its leader. Henry VI soon followed his father to the grave, and a struggle for the throne ensued between Philip the Swabian and Henry's son Otto. The civil war brought destruction to even the most remote regions of the Eifel. Alderic could see many manors and villages which had been burned to the ground.

Two soldiers stopped him at Mechernich, but when they learned that he was the swinekeeper from Fussenich, they burst into laughter. They had thought he resembled the prince of France, and they were heartily amused at their mistake. Alderic was permitted to continue on his journey.

Although Father Herman was pleased that many people requested his services, he was always reluctant to leave his primary responsibility at the abbey to someone else. He told Father Arnulf, "The service of the sacristan is like that performed by Saint Joseph. I am the guardian of the Son of God in the tabernacle. I also prepare His table each day, and I guard the flame of the sanctuary lamp just as Saint Joseph held the lantern in our Savior's manger."

Father Arnulf repeated this to many confreres and, before long, members of the community began calling him "Joseph." The saintly name fit the quiet canon who was known for his purity and pious devotion to Christ and His Mother. The name he had asked his childhood friend Margaret to call him was now respectfully repeated by his confreres in the cloister.

Herman was at first a bit averse to the community's associating him with so holy a man, but soon he was inspired to greater fervor and diligence because of it. He helped with the baking of the hosts to ensure that not a single one was tainted by stain or defect. Water from the well was not pure enough for the altar, so each morning Herman climbed to a spring in the mountain near the monastery. Bad weather never stopped him. Only his clock-repair trips kept him from his duties.

One of the cloister students told Herman of Alderic's arrival saying, "The clock at Fussenich needs fixing again. Women know nothing about such things, but I do. May I go with you, Father Joseph? Please?"

"Of course you may, Wilfrid, if Abbot Ehrenfried permits you."

The abbot consented to the request, not so much for the boy's sake as for the priest's. He had noticed the deep sorrow that often burdened Herman, and he knew that the student's presence would cheer the beloved canon. The cloister students enjoyed a special place in Father Herman's heart, and they deeply admired him as well.

* * *

Wilfrid chattered incessantly on their trip to Fussenich. He had so much to say and so many questions to ask that Father Herman did not get the chance to prepare his spiritual talk for the nuns that evening. Indeed, his ideas were not very well structured, but they reflected the depths of the priest's saintly heart nonetheless, and even the Mother Prioress was spiritually consoled. Margaret struggled to contain her warm feelings of pride during Herman's visit, for she had known the priest as a friend since childhood.

Father Herman fixed the clock again, but he wondered if the Sisters had allowed cats to play among its chains and weights. He had never seen them in such a tangled mess. The Sisters urged him to stay overnight to avoid the dangers of travelling in the darkness, and besides, the old gray horse refused to budge.

During the return trip to Steinfeld the next day, Wilfrid discovered that Alderic was an old Crusader. As the two talked, Herman became absorbed in deep thought. He did not like to hear about the Crusades, which had ended after the tragic death of Frederick Barbarossa. Division among the Crusaders had weakened their campaign, and they lost many lives without achieving their goal. Jerusalem was still controlled by the infidels.

News of Father Egbert's death on the Crusade had recently reached the abbey. Herman learned from Master Nicholas that his troubled friend Peter had joined the Crusade as an act of penance. Herman wondered about his fate as he prayed a fervent *Hail Mary* for him.

Upon their arrival at Steinfeld, Alderic humbly kissed the hand of the canon, who quickly retracted it with surprise. Then he looked at the swinekeeper with such intensity that Alderic felt as if his soul had been read.

"Alderic, you have freely assumed your heavy burden of penance, and God is very pleased with it." Herman's words made Alderic blush, but a joyful sparkle lit up his eyes.

Herman became greatly disturbed when he returned to the church to say a prayer of thanksgiving for the safe journey. Perhaps, he thought, it was a sin of pride to allow others to call him the holy name of Mary's spouse. A fear he could not dismiss told him that he was desecrating the honor of the Holy Family. Herman resolved to ask the abbot about it at the next day's chapter meeting.

As was his custom, Herman faithfully performed his duties that afternoon. He prepared the candles for the dormitory and the altar, and laid out the vestments for the next day's Masses. To his confreres he seemed more quiet and recollected than usual.

\* \* \*

That night, after the others had gone to bed, Herman relished the quiet solitude of the church during the night watch before Matins. Kneeling in a pew at the entrance of the choir, he buried his face in his hands and began to pray. Slowly the noises of the day died down, and a great stillness descended upon the House of God.

Nevertheless a deep restlessness remained in the soul of the solitary canon. The thought which troubled him was that it must be wrong to assume the name 'Joseph' or allow others to call him by it. From the depths of his heart he prayed to the Mother of Good Counsel. The hours passed quickly until the moment when, suddenly, something in the choir startled Herman.

A brilliant light began to fill the entire church with an intensity that nearly blinded Herman's eyes and overwhelmed his soul. The whole choir was filled with radiance and all the candles on the altar were burning. A stream of light was spreading throughout the holy place. His soul seemed to resound with the pealing of bells and he heard singing as if all Heaven had descended to earth. The hand of God once again lifted the enraptured and astonished soul of His servant out of this world and into His own holy light.  "My God, my God!  Tell me what it is you want of me!" the priest exclaimed.

Then Mary appeared, standing at the foot of the high altar, clothed in a regal robe and crowned with stars.  A legion of angels attended her.  Herman had never seen her look so noble and majestic.

One of the assisting angels cried out, "Who will become the spouse of this Virgin?"

And a second angel added, "Who is more worthy than the brother here present?"

"Let him come forward then!" responded the choir of angels.

One of the angels approached the bewildered canon and led him to the heavenly Mother.  The assisting angel continued, "This most pure Virgin is presented to you this day as your Spouse.  Does it please you to marry this illustrious Princess?"

Herman found himself completely unable to respond or move, but a glance from the Virgin assured him.

Then the angel asked him, "For your part, do you consent?"

Herman replied timidly and in ecstasy, "Certainly I do, because *you* desire it, O my Queen, my Mother, and my *Spouse!*"

The assisting angel then placed Herman's hand in Mary's with the words, "She is from this day hence your Spouse, and you will be called Herman *Joseph*."  And the choir of angels sang "*AMEN!*" and cried out, "Long live Herman Joseph, second spouse of the Queen!"

Then Mary tenderly addressed Herman, "Carry my Child just as Joseph bore Him to Egypt.  And since you bear the same burden, you shall also share the same name."  With that, the Virgin placed the Child Jesus in the arms of the enraptured canon.

The priest's body burned inside as though it was being immolated.  His heart was pierced with excruciating pain while, at the same time, it was filled with insurmountable happiness.  He tried to answer, to utter just one word, but his lips were sealed by the grandeur of the miracle.  The holy light dissolved into darkness, yet his arms tingled and his entire being radiated grace.

Then Herman Joseph ran to the tower and, to the surprise of the entire cloister, rang, not the Matins bell, but the heavy bell of Our Lady.

## Chapter Seventeen

# The Golden Rose

**H**erman Joseph opened the door to find Father Anthony seated at his desk holding his head in his hands. He smiled at the man whose deep thoughts he had just disturbed and handed him a rose. "Isn't it beautiful? I thought one of God's loveliest creations would brighten up your cell. Then the illuminated letters in your *Graduale* will be even more beautiful."

"Thank you, Joseph! How kind of you! Perhaps your rose will inspire my illuminations. Once again, I'm hopelessly stuck."

"Don't worry. Your next painting will surely match, if not surpass, the other beautiful letters in this book. The next one always does. Do you know which one is my favorite?" Herman asked.

"It must be the illumination for Christmas: the capital 'P' in *Puer natus est nobis*: 'A child is born to us.' Remember how I painted the crib with Mary, Joseph and an angel in the loop of the 'P'?"

"Yes, that was magnificent. But my favorite is the 'J' from *Jubilate*. *Jubilate Deo omnis terra*: 'Sing joyfully to the Lord, all the earth.' Let's look at it again. See? The angels playing music, the birds singing, the flowers blooming, and people rejoicing. All of God's creation uniting in joyful praise!"

"Yes, it is beautiful. But I was only able to paint it because you gave me the idea. Now I need your help again. I'm working on the Feast of Our Lady's Assumption. *Gaudeamus omnes in Domino*: 'Let us all rejoice in the Lord'. Joseph, what should I do with the capital 'G'? How about an angel holding a censer and bowing deeply?"

"Too serious; not joyful enough. Why don't you interweave the 'G' with a rose? That's it! That's perfect for the Assumption. Mary is the beautiful rose which sprang forth among the thorns of our earthly distress. So God has taken her to heaven as the earth's most beautiful flower. You must paint a rose, Anthony. A golden rose. Wait, I will 'pick' some for you."

Herman returned holding his chalice with the three roses. "Behold the golden roses! The master artist who created the Three Kings' shrine 'grew' these flowers. There are none like them in the whole world!"

"This will inspire the most magnificent illumination in my entire book!" Anthony heartily clasped Herman's hand in appreciation.

* * *

The overwhelming joy Herman Joseph felt was now bearing its most beautiful blossoms. Over and over again his lips uttered the words, "Mary, my rose." He went into the cloister garden which was alive with the splendor of countless roses. This is a greeting from Our Lady, he joyfully thought, and the words of the *Song of Solomon* filled his heart:

> *The winter has passed;*
> *the rains are over and gone;*
> *the flowers appear on the earth.*
> *Open up, my love, my beautiful one, and come!*

The soul of the priest grew increasingly joyful. He entered the church and knelt before the statue of Mary, but he could not express the exuberance which overflowed in his heart. How could his lips give word to the sentiments that flowed through his heart like an unending river! It had been this way ever since the night he had laid his hand in the hand of Mary. His body and soul could not contain the unbearable joy flowing from her love.

While he knelt in prayer, the organ began to play, softly at first, then gradually building to a *crescendo* until the whole church vibrated with resonant jubilation. It was Father Rupert, the greatest master of the organ. Herman Joseph listened to the music, and the happiness of his heart joined in the jubilant, melodious storm. He was filled with the light, the sound, and the joy, and words began to form themselves, words which could never be spoken, words which could only be *sung!* Herman Joseph got up, went to his cell, prayed the *Hail Mary*, and began transcribing with his quill the words that resounded and burned within his soul.

Many hours passed. The sun had already set and cast its golden rays into the cell of the priest. He finally laid down his quill and took his work to Father Anthony's room.

"I have finished the rose," declared the artist happily as he laid down his brush.

Herman Joseph silently studied the painting with great delight. Then he said, "My heart has also sung to the Heavenly Rose this day. Listen:"

*Gaude, plaude, clara Rosa!*
*Esto moesto cara prosa.*
*Salutanti, supplicanti,*
*Te roganti, dic amanti.*
*In Christo: te servavero.*

*Rejoice, applaud, O fairest rose!*
*Be for the sad a comforting prose.*
*Deign now to speak to him who greets you,*
*To him who loves you and implores you.*
*In Christ ever will I serve you.*

The red glow of evening grew brighter and bathed the cell in light as the song continued:

*Rejoice, O Queen, whose diadem*
*Glows with the gifts of saints as gem,*
*Whose splendid radiance glows like flame.*
*How great your honor, how worthy of fame!*
*Who could further sing your praise?*

*Rejoice, whose love is manifest*
*As a powerful cry within the breast.*
*Love, whose presence is truly proven*
*By a lance in a side laid open.*
*The anguished soul in suffering burns.*

*Rejoice, rejoice, O Full of Grace!*
*What I have drunk – how sweet the taste!*
*To him who seeks you is eternity shown,*
*The one you love shall be your own.*
*How blessed is he who follows you!*

From the church the music of the organ began to play again and fill the cell. And Herman continued his beauteous song of praise to the Holy Mother:

*Rejoice, O sweetest nightingale,*
*Whose voice so full of love, I hail!*
*Rejoice, you fairest, sweetest song,*
*In the lofty praise of the saintly throng,*
*The pleasure of all and angelic joy.*

*Rejoice, O Queen, with roses crowned,*
*Bedecked with flowers your radiant gown.*
*The sparkling splendor of your holy attire*
*Glorifies light, enkindles the fire,*
*Adorns the blessed heavenly court.*

Verse after verse rang out. The evening glow died down. The stars rose in the heavens and Herman continued without looking at the parchment any more.

*Rejoice, O shining star of the sea,*
*The Divine Light's mother, rejoice to see*
*The awesome splendor of the warming sun,*
*And contemplate God Three-in-One*
*In all His beauty and majesty.*

*Rejoice, whose face gives a smile of gold.*
*How blessed the man who can behold;*
*Enchanted, enraptured, he stands to admire,*
*With burning devotion he is set on fire,*
*Wounded by your overpowering love.*

*Rejoice, O Maiden, pure and chaste,*
*Our royal Master's dwelling place,*
*Under whose mantle no trembling comes*
*To poor and wretched little ones,*
*For there the timid find their shelter.*

*Rejoice, O Rose, most precious, most fair,*
*To whom no other rose can compare.*
*Singular rose of all roses are you,*
*You, the only rose that is true.*
*O, lovely violet, heavenly lily!*

The cell grew very dark, but still the song to the Blessed Mother went on:

*Come, O Sweetest, enter my home,*
*And bring with you the Beloved One,*
*For I aspire to make you my guest.*
*In me, O Fairest, take your rest.*
*In your great love, consider me.*

*Embrace me, O delight of mine*
*With loving hands, so pure and fine,*
*That I may come to love you best,*
*And loving you, I may not rest.*
*Be for me my soul's reward!*

*Rejoice, inviolate, ever-near,*
*My own prayers please deign to hear.*
*Rejoice with overflowing bliss!*
*May the praises of my littleness*
*Resound always within your ears.*

*Rest, O precious, blessed one,*
*And dawn within me like the sun;*
*Into your care myself I commend.*
*Pardon my weakness when I offend*
*In the light of day or dark of night.*

There was a long silence between the two canons, as if they were savoring the song's afterglow. Then Father Anthony took Herman Joseph's hand and said, "God has inspired your wondrous song." He took up the page of his illuminated *Graduale* and lamented, "See how my rose is completely faded! We can no longer see it. Besides, what is its gold compared with the magnificence of your rose!"

Then Herman Joseph picked up a candle which stood before the statue of Mary, lit it, and placed it on the desk by the painting. "See, my brother, now your rose glows once again in the light of Our Lady!" And both canons gazed at the radiance of the golden rose.

Herman Joseph spent the hours of his night watch kneeling before the statue of the Blessed Virgin. He offered up all the joys of the day for those whose hearts were sad and troubled.

The sound of a traveler at the cloister gate called him from his prayers. He went to the sacristy, lit a lantern, and opened the gate. In the dim light, he saw a pitiful man with shabby clothes and a pale face. A poor sufferer, thought the canon, who seeks shelter in a house of charity.

"Please enter in the name of Christ!" Herman Joseph welcomed the stranger, who quietly followed him to one of the guestrooms.

But the priest had hardly lit a few candles when the guest cried out, "Herman! It's me! Please don't throw me out!"

"Peter!" said the priest, trembling. "You've finally returned. I have waited so long for you."

"You have?"

"Yes. I knew you'd come back. Come, sit down. I will bring you something to eat and drink. Have you traveled far?"

"Yes, far, very far. I went the way of evil, as you know, but I've made amends, Herman. I have suffered much." Peter sat down on a stool and cradled his head in his hands. When he spoke again, it was almost inaudible.

"The last time I was here you opened the door for me, Herman. And I fled into the night. I tried to get away from my companions, from myself, my conscience, but I found no peace. Day and night I saw your eyes looking at me, so full of love and sadness. It was worse than looking into the cold eyes of the hangman."

Peter paused briefly to catch his breath. Beads of sweat appeared on his forehead as he continued, "I had to make amends, to erase the evil and replace it with goodness. So I set out with the Crusade and fought in many battles among the first ranks. I yearned to be killed or at least suffer some wound, even a small wound, as a sign that God had accepted my penance. But no arrows struck me, no sword even grazed my flesh. The Crusade ended in failure, and I returned home uninjured. In my soul I believed that God had turned away from me; that He had refused to acknowledge my offering."

He put his hand to his damp forehead. Herman Joseph wanted to say a word of comfort, but before he could, Peter continued, "So I searched for another way to do penance. I wandered to Speyer where the people were rebuilding the cathedral that had burnt down thirty years before. I asked the builders to let me work with them. I wanted to appease God's anger by helping to raise this house in His honor. From sunrise to sunset, I hauled stones to the building site until my hands became sore and bloody. Every day I was the first to arrive and the last to leave, and I did the heaviest work I could, all for no wages except my daily bread. But it wasn't enough. Still there was no peace. Your eyes still haunted me, Herman."

Peter paused again. Then, sighing, he continued: "The cathedral was finally near completion, and the cross had to be placed on the dome. I asked if I could carry it to the top, Herman. I thought that I could do my penance by carrying that cross. The strain was beyond measure because the cross was extremely heavy. Suddenly everything became dark and my hands gripped emptiness. I *fell*, Herman, and I just kept falling. I will never forget the emptiness of falling. Fortunately, I got caught in some scaffolding. For a while I hung there, suspended between heaven and earth like the thief on Golgotha. How long, I can't remember. I only know what I thought about during those minutes of terror: I believed that God had thrown me down from the cross.

"Then my clothes ripped, and I fell swiftly to the ground. I could hear the screams of the crowd which had gathered near the Cathedral. Then I experienced pain worse than I had ever felt and I passed out.

"I awoke in a hospital. For a long time I hung between life and death. But I survived and eventually healed. I had to learn to reuse my damaged limbs. It was a slow and excruciatingly painful process. But at last my limbs were fully healed.

"I've come to you, Herman, though, because there is still here within me a wound that will not heal. Tell me the truth, Herman, I beg you. Did God cast me down because I raised His cross in arrogance? Or has He accepted my penance?"

With a gentle grip, Herman pulled the hands of the penitent apart and said, "Peter, you know the words Jesus spoke to the thief who was filled with contrition. We learned them together at the parish school. Remember those words?"

"*Amen, amen, I say to you. This day you will be with Me in Paradise,*" Peter said reflectively.

117

"So be comforted, Peter. Do not question any further. God has heard you, too," said Herman.

Peter threw himself onto his knees, covered his face with his hands, and began to cry. He cried for the first time since childhood. His tears contained the years of suffering he had endured, and shedding them brought tremendous relief. Herman Joseph left the room to get some bread and wine, and, upon returning, he found his old friend's face filled with peace instead of anguish.

"Come, Peter, eat and drink! I will find a job for you, and if worse comes to worst, you can stay here at the abbey."

When Peter had finished his meal, Herman urged him to come along: "Someone is waiting for you, Peter."

"Who could be waiting for *me*?" Peter asked.

"Your *Mother*, Peter. Do you remember how we used to explore the churches of Cologne in search of true greatness and nobility?"

"How could I ever forget?"

"You will find true greatness and nobility in the heart of our heavenly Mother!"

They proceeded to the church and knelt before the statue of the Blessed Virgin. After some time spent in silent prayer, the priest sang out with profound joy:

> *Rejoice, inviolate, ever-near,*
> *My own prayers kindly deign to hear.*
> *Rejoice with overflowing bliss!*
> *May the praises of my littleness*
> *Ever resound within your ears.*
>
> *Rest, O precious blessed one,*
> *And dawn within me like the sun;*
> *Into your care myself I commend.*
> *Pardon my weakness when I offend*
> *In the light of day or dark of night.*

The glimmering light of the stars danced against the church windows, and the eternal flame in the sanctuary lamp glowed like a brilliant red rose.

## Chapter Eighteen
# The Pharisee and the Publican

**M**aster Nicholas' gloomy thoughts contrasted sharply with the joyful spring day. He despaired that the shrine of the Three Kings would ever be finished. It was not a lack of inspiration that delayed its completion, but a lack of money. The artist's funds had been exhausted, and no more would be available until Cologne had finished repairing its city walls.

The Rhineland had also suffered much in the past year, 1205. The civil war, which continued between Otto the Guelf and Philip the Hohenstaufen, produced an endless harvest of destruction, death, and misery. The civil and religious strife also inspired much treachery and deception.

Adolph, the archbishop of Cologne, had abandoned his allegiance to Otto and had solemnly crowned Philip as emperor of Germany. The citizens of Cologne, however, remained loyal to the Guelf. When Pope Innocent III excommunicated Adolph, the city supported its new bishop, Bruno von Sayn, the former abbot of the Cassius Monastery in Bonn. Adolph would not be so easily dismissed, however. Troops loyal to him raided and plundered the city. Adolph's cousin, Engelbert von Berg, led these ruthless campaigns.

Such were the depressing thoughts which filled the mind of the master goldsmith when, all of a sudden, a loud bang at his door pulled him from their morass. A man dressed in splendid attire introduced himself, "I am Stephen, the wealthy merchant who built the castle above the Rhine. Surely you have heard of me."

"What do you want from me?" Nicholas answered curtly.

"I have a commission for you: a golden necklace with many precious stones for my wife. The cost doesn't matter."

"I cannot take your commission. I do not make worldly jewelry. All my work is religious."

"My, you *are* strange! These are difficult times to make such money as this. Another goldsmith would not pass up such an opportunity. But I wanted to commission the creator of the Three Kings' shrine. There's the masterpiece! What a great work of art!

"Say, you've put famous faces on many of the holy figures. Moses – that's the brother of the doorkeeper of Saint Pantaleon's.

And Jonah – that's Dean Ensfried of Saint Andrew. Didn't he recently take his pants right out from under his habit and give them to a cold beggar?"

"He is a very holy man!" the artist sternly asserted.

Stephen only snickered, "Saints are all very strange people. But tell me, who is this under the cloverleaf arch? The wealthy King Solomon?"

"The *wise* King Solomon!" Nicholas corrected him.

"Sir, I have a proposal for you. I will provide you with a sum of money large enough to complete this masterpiece. All I ask is that you use my face for King Solomon."

"I cannot accept your offer."

"Why, in heaven's name, not?"

"Because your money is too dirty for me! This shrine will not be completed with tainted gold and silver!"

"How dare you call my money dirty!"

"Didn't you profit from the Crusades?"

"I helped outfit the Crusaders, and that's a good deed!"

"A good deed, yes, and much better business. Countless soldiers died while you got rich." Indignation boiled within the merchant, but Master Nicholas continued. "During the famine of 1197 you exploited the poor and the weak to continue enlarging your moneybags. You disregarded their plight for your own profit!"

"Now wait a minute, sir!"

"I'm not finished yet. Then the civil war broke out, and you saw another opportunity to profit by selling weapons. But you sold them to both sides! You increased your profit, as well as the destruction and killing. And now you want to pay me with money minted from men's misery? Your gold is too dirty for me. Good day, Sir!"

\* \* \*

The merchant left the workshop pale, shaking, and rendered speechless by rage. He had never been so humiliated. Stephen was still seething with fury when he returned to his castle and found a man in a white habit waiting for him.

"Hello, *Sultan*."

"Who are you?" Stephen answered indignantly.

"Father Herman from Steinfeld."

"Of course! Now I recognize you," the merchant exclaimed. His fury slowly gave way to curiosity. "What brings you here?"

120

"Remember how we used to sit on the banks of the Rhine and dream about our future? You said you'd be rich. You'd have a castle above the river with a cellar filled with gold."

"And I was right," Stephen boastfully responded. "And what about you?"

"Remember that I said there is something more exalted than gold?"

"Did you find it?"

"Yes. True greatness and nobility, through holiness. But there was a third person with us: Peter of Heaven Street. He said..."

"Don't talk to me about that tramp, that bandit!" Stephen shouted abruptly. "It's too bad the executioner can't touch him because he was in the Crusade! Let's change the subject, Herman."

"No, I want to talk to you about Peter! He has suffered very much. He came to me a few days ago a changed man. That's why I've paid you this visit. Please take Peter in and give him some work in your warehouses."

"Surely you jest!" Stephen laughed mockingly. "Take in that scoundrel, that robber, so that he can plunder my castle?"

"Peter has done penance, Stephen. We shouldn't continue to hold his past faults against him. What about our own faults? Remember, *whoever among you is without fault, let him cast the first stone!*"

"*Without fault?!*" Stephen blurted venomously. "I'm no angel, but thanks be to God I'm no robber or murderer. I have a wife and child to care for. I can't look after every delinquent who comes along. Look under that tree, Herman. That's my son Martin. He's only seven, but already he can read.

"Come here, Martin, and shake hands with Father Herman." The boy came to his father carrying a book. "Now, read something for him. What book do you have? The Bible! Fine! Read something from the Bible."

The boy read aloud in a clear voice:

*The Pharisee stood there and prayed, 'Oh God, I thank You that I am not like other men, like robbers, cheaters, adulterers, or even like this Publican here!'*

"That's fine, son. That's enough," interrupted the red-faced merchant.

"Listen to what the child has read, Stephen. Then consider once again what I've asked. God be with you!"

"Yes, yes, goodbye!" Stephen responded, anxious to see his old friend leave.

"May God not punish you through your son for your arrogance ," Herman said as he departed.

For the second time that day, the merchant became outraged.

* * *

Two days later Herman Joseph returned home from his long journey. He arrived late at night and had scarcely settled into his room when the wagon of the Sisters from Fussenich rattled through the abbey gate.

"Their clock has stopped again!" sighed the priest, smiling to himself. But Herman knew something else was wrong, because Alderic was not driving the wagon. The convent servant told the priest that the swinekeeper was dying and had asked for him. The priest readied himself immediately, and Peter insisted on travelling with them in case they encountered any danger.

They arrived at the Norbertine convent in the pre-dawn light. Herman Joseph went directly to the miserable hut of the swinekeeper, who, though feverish, looked at the priest with gleaming eyes. "You have come, Father Herman!"

"Love should never make misery wait," answered the priest as he wiped the dying man's forehead.

"I have a grave sin I want to confess. I desecrated the Crusades because I was inspired by ambition and greed, not by love of Christ."

Herman Joseph listened to the dying man with heavenly compassion. "You have sinned, and you have done penance. God has looked favorably upon your sacrifice, Alderic. Your sins are forgiven you." Then he made the sign of the cross of absolution over the dying man.

Alderic lay quietly with his eyes closed for a long time. Then he looked up at the priest and said, "I have something else to tell you. I have served here for many years, but no one knows who I really am. I have used a false name. Please send the news to my father that his son died in God's peace, doing penance. He does not know where I am."

"Who is your father?" Herman asked.

"The King of France," the repentant swinekeeper responded.

Herman was stunned by this disclosure, although his intuition had sensed something special within the humble swinekeeper. He promised to fulfill the dying man's wish. Then Herman brought *Viaticum* to Alderic, who passed away peacefully in the priest's arms.

The Sisters were understandably shaken by the death of their loyal servant. "He was so faithful and reliable," said the Mother Superior. "Where will we ever find another like him?"

Herman Joseph then looked at his old friend Peter, whose glowing face showed that he had experienced the same illumination.

"If I am not too lowly for the honorable Sisters," Peter stuttered.

"Mother Jepa," Herman said, "I am sure that you will find Peter to be a most reliable and loyal servant."

So the penitential work continued among the pigs of Fussenich, and Father Herman Joseph returned to the abbey of Steinfeld alone.

## Chapter Nineteen
# The Storm of Youth

The beauty of the spring morning in the year 1212 was lost on Father Rudolph, who walked through the cloister courtyard immersed in his conversation with Father Arnulf.

"Something has gotten into my boys," the teacher complained. "They were always so well disciplined, but now they are unruly. No one cares about his studies any more, not even for the beautiful stories of Cornelius Nepos!"

"It's not that bad, is it?" The corpulent confrere was trying to comfort his brother. He was growing tired from trying to keep up with the taller canon while talking at the same time. The strides of the two men resembled those of the wanderer dactyl: long, short-short. "Boys have always been that way, especially with the approach of warmer weather. A mouse eats paper only in times of greatest need. It would rather have a piece of bacon. It's the same with your boys."

"It's much more serious than that, my dear confrere. A French lad arrived a few days ago. He told the boys about a 'Crusade of Children.' He told them what a pity it was that the tomb of Our Lord has remained in the hands of the infidels. He said they, the children, could help accomplish the goal which had eluded their fathers. So yesterday, in the middle of class, one of my boys slammed his book shut and announced that this was no time for fairy tales. He said it was the time to march! And, just imagine, Arnulf, everyone else applauded him!"

"Maybe it's just a touch of spring fever," Arnulf proposed with a gasp.

"I tried to expel that fever with my rod, but to no avail. It only made them more recalcitrant."

"You're absolutely right there, Rudolph!" interjected Father Anthony, who had overheard his confrere's complaint. "The rod cannot extinguish the flame which burns within youthful hearts. I've just returned from Cologne, and things there are even more chaotic. Children are leaving their families and running away from their homes. They're stealing weapons and tools and anything they think will help them fight for the Holy Land."

"What got them stirred up?" groaned the teacher.

"They heard the same preaching from wandering monks about a Crusade that their fathers heard. But while their parents paused to consider the cost, the young people just rose up and set out."

Just then, the three priests heard the sounds of a skirmish, and so they hurried across the courtyard to the growing crowd of students. They were surrounding Abbot Macarius and accosting him with bellicose gestures, fierce glares, and angry shouts.

"Father Abbot, we do not ask, we *demand* dismissal and your blessing for the Crusade." It was Wilfrid, the *quadrivium* spokesman.

"You have no right to speak to me that way!" thundered the abbot.

"I have the right of one called by Christ!"

The swarm of students clamored in approval. "We, the sons of Norbert, will not remain behind while the rest of Germany's youth liberate the tomb of Our Lord!"

"Our founder first demands obedience from his sons!" the abbot responded.

"We obey God over men! And God has called us, Father Abbot, so you can't stop us!"

"Prove that your calling is divine!" challenged the abbot over the din.

"*Prove?!* Must one prove with words something that consumes the heart and burns within the breast?! Hear the proof in our heartfelt cries, Father Abbot! In lands everywhere, the cry of the youth is sounding! It must be God's will!"

"Are you sure it's not your own pride and self-deception?"

"If only Father Joseph were here," Father Anthony whispered to Father Arnulf. "He knows how to speak to the boys like no one else."

"Yes, but he's gone to Hoven again to fix the convent clock."

Wilfrid then announced, "Father Abbot, if you refuse to give us dismissal and your blessing, then we will leave without them. Come on, brothers! Break open the armory! Take sickles, pitchforks, cudgels, and whips! Onward in the name of Christ!" The band of boys echoed his cry.

The canons were too few to restrain the mob, and the boys armed themselves with the tools from the sheds. Before long, one boy announced the approach of other Crusaders from Trier and Eifel.

125

In the distance, one could hear the swelling strains of a battle song, inspiring the youths to liberate the Holy Sepulcher:

*Now we march as we follow our call!*
*Arm yourselves lest you fall,*
*And be armed by Faith most of all,*
*That we may earn our eternal reward!*

*God will end sorrow throughout all lands;*
*He will do it with our hands!*
*Disgrace will not come upon our bands,*
*For we have with us the Holy Ghost!*

Hearing this song, the young sons of Norbert raised their weapons, shouted greetings to their approaching comrades, and soon joined the growing ranks of the children's army. Before long, the abbey grounds were deathly quiet.

"No one has stayed behind," marveled Father Anthony. "This truly is a holy storm of youth."

"No, this is an *unholy* storm," the abbot retorted. "There is no obedience here. God always speaks to young people through their elders. This is contrary to God's command."

Herman Joseph learned of the boys' departure upon his arrival from Hoven. His face grew white and he faltered as if shaken by a tremendous physical blow. Then he gathered himself and spoke:

"This had to come. And we adults are to blame! We disgraced the Crusades with our ambition, so now the children have set out with pure hearts."

"Do not defend the boys," warned Abbot Macarius. "This is nothing but a rebellion against the Fourth Commandment!"

"I did not say they have done right; but their will, their intention, was good. We are the ones who did not recognize the flaming storm in their hearts and guide them in the right direction. So they have become strangers to us, following not our words but the storm in their hearts. And this storm they call divine inspiration. Father Abbot, you let them leave without your blessing?"

"Should I have blessed them in their misdeed?!"

"Those who stray are most in need of a blessing. Our boys are headed for great suffering. We must pray and sacrifice for them!"

* * *

Herman Joseph then entered the church and cast himself down before the image of the Blessed Mother. He implored her for help and pleaded to God with heartfelt sorrow. Herman spent seemingly endless days afterward being tortured by grief and abandonment. He was almost constantly prostrate before Mary's statue: "Why, Mother, why have you permitted this? Why?!"

Then the image of the joyful Mother with her Child was transformed into Our Lady of Sorrows, holding the lifeless body of her Son: "God has not spared His only Son, but has given Him up in death for us all." Then Herman understood the penitential nature of the Children's Crusade. "Lord, Thy will be done!"

Several days later Herman Joseph was called to the parlor to receive a guest. It was Stephen, his boyhood friend. Herman immediately sensed that sitting before him was not the arrogant and self-righteous merchant of former days, but a poor man humbled by God. Stephen grasped the priest's hands and fell to his knees.

"What did you say when you recently left me in anger?" Stephen asked.

"In sorrow, not in anger, Stephen," Herman Joseph corrected him.

"Didn't you say that God would punish my arrogance through my son? Oh God, you have spoken the truth!"

"Stephen, what's the matter with Martin?"

"He has run off with the Crusaders! I tried to lock him up to prevent him from running away, but it was useless. And when I finally found him in the children's army, I tried to force him to come home. But the other boys surrounded him and raised their weapons against me. They would've killed me before handing Martin over! I watched helplessly as my boy marched away."

"It is God's punishment, Stephen. You wanted to make him a good merchant, but your son's soul was longing for truly great and heroic things. Your boy became a stranger to you, such that no lock or bolt could hold him back."

"Yes, but what should I do?" wailed the grieving father. "Something must be done. I can't sit quietly while my son rushes to his ruin!"

"It's time to pray and do penance."

"You're right, Father Herman. But what should I do? Tell me. Is Peter still here? I want to take him in. I want to make reparation for my sins of pride."

"Someone else took Peter in a long time ago."

"So what should I do then? I want to do a good work to get my son back home safely. I would like to help someone in need."

"You could give money to Master Nicholas so he can complete the shrine of the Three Kings," Herman Joseph suggested.

"He won't take it. He said he didn't want my 'dirty money.'"

"Then purify it. Repay what you have acquired unjustly before you make an offering for the shrine. As long as you offer the money in a real spirit of penance, Nicholas will not refuse you. True penance washes away any guilt."

"And you think God will accept my sacrifice and return my son?"

"You can't bargain with God, Stephen! What He gives you, He gives out of pure grace."

"So what consolation can you offer me, Herman?"

"*I* can't give you any, but someone else can."

"Who?"

"Our Mother of Good Counsel! Come with me, my friend."

They entered the abbey church and knelt before the statue of Mary. After much time spent in deep prayer, Herman Joseph spoke aloud: "Mother, show us your goodness. We are overcome with distress. But distress is your time, for all distress cries to the Mother. Your time has arrived, Blessed Lady. Forget us not, dear Mother, and treat us according to your tenderness!"

# Chapter Twenty
# The Time of the Mother

Thank you, Albert. Thank you from the bottom of my heart!" Herman Joseph held a curious string of beads which Father Albert had brought back from France. "Yes, this is a most fitting tribute to Our Lady: a garland of roses, a string of pearls. Each prayer is a priceless gem we offer to our Blessed Mother."

"I knew you would appreciate it," Albert responded. "They say that a holy friar assembled this 'string of pearls' as you call it. He wanders throughout Southern France preaching to the Albigensian heretics and to all the ignorant. He owns nothing and must depend on alms and charity for his bread and his lodging. He has endured much ridicule, scorn, and even violence, but he blesses those who abuse him."

"What is his name?" Herman Joseph asked.

"Dominic. He is Castilian. When he was a student in Valencia, he gave away all his possessions to the poor. He even sold his books to buy meals for the hungry. He said, 'Why should I brood over books when my brother is dying from hunger?'"

"He must be a very holy man," Herman Joseph said. He was deeply moved. He imagined, in his mind's eye, this powerful preacher. "And he was the one who originated this prayer, the *Rosary*?"

"Yes. Like him, it is very simple yet profound. There is much more than the repetition of the *Hail Mary*. The Rosary is a window to the lives of Our Lord and Our Lady."

"How true, Albert. We are only children before God. Our prayers should have the ring of simplicity to them, like a child before his mother. Once again, Albert, I can't thank you enough for your gift. But tell me, how is Engelbert, the provost of Cologne? Didn't he join the Crusade to France?"

"Yes. He answered Pope Innocent's call to fight the Albigensian rebels, and he returned home a different man than the hot-tempered nobleman from earlier times. They say he met with Dominic. That is what must have changed his heart. You know the See of Cologne is vacant. It is rumored that Engelbert will be the next archbishop."

"I hope you are right about his change of heart. May God grant to Cologne a good bishop!"

Herman Joseph then walked to the church to pray his very first Rosary.

* * *

News of the fate of the Children's Crusade began to arrive. Thousands of youths had perished in the wilderness from fever, pestilence, cold, and accidents. Only one-third of the children survived the first few months.

At home in Germany, hearts cried out in sorrow to the Mother of God. Never had so many candles burned before the statues of Mary. Passion plays were performed outside church doors, and the cries from the Cross and the lamentations of Mary resounded more emotionally than ever before.

A new scene was added to the passion play in which Christ's dead body was laid across His Mother's lap. Herman Joseph had witnessed that very sight in the solitude of his prayers. Mary assumed the role of the Mother of Sorrows in order to invite those who were suffering to enter into her own pierced heart.

* * *

It was now the year 1215, and the aging Father Herman Joseph no longer needed to fix clocks in order to visit the convents of the Eifel. He went to these cloisters regularly to celebrate Mass and preach to the nuns. The Cistercian nuns were listening to his inspired words during one especially memorable visit:

"You share pure virginity with our Immaculate Queen," he preached. "But you also share in her motherhood as well. You are the real mothers of the poor, the troubled, the orphans, the aged, and of all who cry for motherly counsel and help.

"You are like the Blessed Lady in her suffering. Mary stood under the Cross, and I know that each of you quietly bears her own. Each day God gives you a cup, and you fill it with much toil and grief. When you have filled the cup at the end of each day, raise it to the Lord and say, 'I give You this day,' just as Mary did with the daily offerings of her own life.

"Sisters, you are the mothers of the world. The world desperately needs you just as a child needs his mother, and never before has the world needed you so much. Our time of sorrow is truly the time of the Mother!"

Father Herman Joseph then led the Sisters in praying the Rosary to Our Lady of Sorrows. A knocking at the cloister door momentarily interrupted their prayerful chant, but the priest urged the Sisters to continue praying while he answered it.

A small group of young and battered wanderers stood before the priest at the open door. His face lit up with surprise and joy as he realized who they were. He extended his arms to the weary homecomers. Their faces, however, remained gloomy and their eyes downcast. Not one sought the priest's embrace.

"Is this all who have returned?" Herman Joseph asked a bit fearfully. None of the youths responded. The priest covered his face with his trembling hands before he composed himself and continued: "Where are you going?" he asked.

"We are going to Steinfeld," answered one of the youths. Herman Joseph thought he recognized him except for the mournful countenance and the weakened spirit. It was Wilfrid. "We want to return to Steinfeld and ask the abbot for a strict judgment."

"You will be received with love and mercy at Steinfeld," Herman Joseph assured him.

"I don't want mercy! I have seen too many perish who had set out so full of hope. And I am the guilty one. They are on my conscience!"

"You did not lead them," Herman Joseph said, putting his arm around Wilfrid's shoulder. "God has led them."

"God did not cause this suffering. That's blasphemy, Father!"

"God did not spare even His only Son. You wanted to make a Crusade. God led you along the way of the Cross. You marched to fight for the Faith, and God chose you to carry His Cross. You have atoned for much of the guilt of our times."

Wilfrid's face turned quizzical before it began to brighten. "We have atoned for sins? We thought our efforts were in vain, especially when the bishop of Brindisi sent us home like children."

"Nothing is in vain. Neither your sorrow, nor the death of your brothers. God will bestow His grace upon us because of your sufferings."

Hearing this, many of the youngsters broke into sobs. Then Herman Joseph led them into the church where the Cistercian nuns were still praying the Rosary. They stopped abruptly when they saw the tattered band of boys.

"Look here, my children!" the priest joyfully announced. "Your journey was not in vain. Because of you, men have learned to find their Mother again!"

The canons of Steinfeld received the homecomers with a tremendous outpouring of love. The abbot uttered no harsh words. On the contrary, he hugged each one as if he had never left. And the young boys' hearts slowly began to mend.

* * *

Several days later, Herman Joseph was called again to the parlor where Stephen sat before him. As the merchant struggled to stand and hold himself erect, the priest looked into his eyes and knew everything without even asking.

"Did your son die in honor?"

"Yes. He was one of the last to die. They buried him with their banner."

Herman Joseph reached for his friend with trembling hands and then held him in silence. After a while the merchant continued:

"Others have returned home, but my boy is dead. I have nothing of value left in this world. I can now give away all my riches to the poor. I have no heir; my son is dead!"

"Stephen, your boy is not dead. He walked the Way of the Cross with Christ. Now Mary has taken his body into her lap. Whoever Mary takes to herself will rise to eternal life!"

After a long silence, the quivering lips of the lonely father repeated these last words of the priest.

## Chapter Twenty One
# Signs in Heaven

The great shrine of the Three Kings was completed and found its place in the Cathedral of Cologne. The numerous votive candles which burned before it created dazzling effects upon its many precious jewels. Each candle represented a prayer to the Holy Magi. There were candles of thanksgiving for the sons who returned and candles of mourning for those who did not.

Darkness and silence now enveloped the great cathedral, which earlier that day had been filled with people, light and music. It had been a bitterly cold day, but one of celebration and rejoicing nevertheless, for February 29, 1216, was the day Count Engelbert von Berg was installed as the new archbishop of Cologne.

A few hours after the ceremony he returned to kneel in prayer before the venerable shrine: "Before this holy shrine I pledge to wield my crosier and scepter with wisdom and benevolence, according to justice and the law. I pledge to protect the welfare of my children and their Church, which glorifies God and follows His laws. Give me your kingly wisdom, O you three holy ones. You did not kneel before an earthly king but sought only the newborn King of heaven!

"I pledge to build a new cathedral over this shrine. It shall be like no other in the German Empire: a royal cathedral above this shrine of kings. But I will consecrate this cathedral to Our Lady. Before her the three kings laid down their crowns. Grant, O Lord, that I may complete this holy work!"

\* \* \*

That same night Herman Joseph stood at the top of the north tower and gazed up at the radiant sky. The night's clarity enabled him to see over the hills of the Eifel all the way to Cologne. Its darkness provided a stunning backdrop for the brilliant stars.

"The stars rest like a burning crown over the royal city," he said in the vast stillness. Then he remembered that, on that very day, a new head had assumed the Church's spiritual crown. "Lord, give your flock a good shepherd," he prayed.

He continued to gaze, transfixed, into the sky while he pondered more deeply its celestial lights. Could they be God's lamps of consolation for those drowning in darkness? He recalled with a smile how he used to explain to little Margaret that the stars were holes in the floor of heaven. Then he was filled with a great yearning to see deeper into the miracle of creation: "Lord, let me look into the shining secrets of your firmament. Lord, let me see!"

All of a sudden, the sky lit up. Stars began falling, so that it looked like burning rain. Herman's heart blazed with a thousand flames. He cried out in agony. His eyes were almost blinded, yet he could not turn away. Stars grew into suns, which consumed all of creation in a rotating, flaming, jubilant song of light.

Herman continued to search deeper into the meaning of this immense immolation. He had to know what was at its heart. Then the answer came, as though from the deepest depths within him:

"The heart of all the world is Love!"

* * *

That same night, another holy man, Francis, stood in the Umbrian hills of Italy and marveled at the sparkling sky. His heart was also consumed by a flaming joy that impelled him to sing out:

*Praised be You, my Lord,*
*In all Your creatures,*
*Especially for Brother Sun,*
*Who makes the day and enlightens us through You.*
*He is lovely and radiant and grand;*
*And he heralds You, Most High Lord.*

*Praised be You, my Lord,*
*For Sister Moon and for the stars.*
*You have hung them in heaven*
*Shining and precious and fair.*

In Umbria, in the Eifel, and the entire world over, the ineffable song of jubilation resounded within the hearts of saints.

* * *

Just as he had promised in his prayer before the Three Kings' shrine, Engelbert proved to be a just and compassionate archbishop. He banished the jugglers, jesters and flatterers who strutted around every other court of the time. The needs of the poor were his central concern. He knew the poor were often deterred from seeking justice

134

because of the high costs of court, so he frequently heard their pleas himself. Many protested that this procedure undermined the city's laws, but Engelbert asserted that the rights of the poor were more important than mere words on dusty parchment.

He developed a reputation for inviting beggars to dine with him and for delaying his own plans when someone in need approached him. On one occasion a poor man came to him with a plea just as he was preparing to ride. Immediately Engelbert swung out of his saddle and heard the man's case on the spot. Another time, in Westphalia, Engelbert was preparing to eat dinner when a woman appeared in the hall with her children, weeping bitterly. A local robber baron had killed her husband and forced her and her children off their land. At this, Engelbert sprang up.

"Mount!" he shouted to the members of his entourage. "It is not right for the shepherd to feast while the flock starves." And turning to the woman he added, "Sit down at my table with your children. This meal is prepared for you. In the meantime, we will try, with the help of God, to restore your rights." Then Engelbert rode off with his retinue, stormed the castle of the wicked man, hanged him from the castle gate, and returned to the widow her rightful property. The archbishop's hand was one which blessed but also one which could strike a necessary blow.

Engelbert invited the followers of Saint Francis and Saint Dominic to Cologne and gave them lands for their cloisters. Soon the brothers of poverty were often seen walking throughout the city's streets and preaching in its churches.

The archbishop did not forget his other promise, although he rejected the architects' first plans for the new cathedral.

"That is not the royal cathedral which will honor Our Lady. Make new plans, gentlemen!"

* * *

As Engelbert's reputation for piety and strength grew, so did his power within the German Empire. He was already the most powerful prince in Germany when the new emperor, Frederick II, named Engelbert to be the administrator of the empire during his absence. The powerful prince-bishop worked even harder to protect the welfare of those under his care.

On one occasion, a merchant requested protection for a caravan passing over the Harz Mountains. "Just show this to any ambushing bandits," Engelbert said, giving the man his glove. More than once the glove proved its might and after the successful trip the merchant wrote:

"My lord, with your protection I will travel through the thickest forest, even travel to the land of the Muslims, where Christendom has long since ended."

* * *

Engelbert's sense of justice knew no bounds and favored no one, not even his own relatives. A complaint was once brought before the bishop against his nephew, Count Frederick of Isenburg. He had been exploiting the monastery at Essen, which as its guardian he should have been protecting. Engelbert removed him from his lucrative position after forcing Frederick to make reparation to the Essen monks.

After a long period of bitterness, Engelbert hoped to reconcile with his nephew. He planned to consecrate a church in Schwelm in November of 1225, and there he hoped to meet with Count Frederick.

The morning of his departure arrived. The archbishop was mounting his horse when a figure in a white habit pressed through the crowd. The cleric was old and thin. He approached the archbishop, grabbed his reins, and cried out, "My lord, do not ride to Schwelm!"

The bishop blazed with anger, but when he looked into the pleading eyes of the elderly priest, he restrained himself. Then he asked if anyone knew the canon.

"He is the Premonstratensian Herman Joseph from Steinfeld," answered a priest in the entourage. "In the cloisters of the Eifel he is called 'the saint.'"

"What urgent message causes you to grab my reins?"

"Do not ride to Schwelm!" Herman repeated. "I implore you, for the sake of your bishopric, for the sake of the empire, do not go! Men are waiting to ambush you!"

"Who lies in wait for me? Who would dare do such a thing?"

"*Death*," Herman Joseph answered.

"Perhaps you have some information regarding a conspiracy against my life. Please tell me."

"I have no news, but a strange premonition has disturbed my heart. My lord, believe the wisdom of an old man. I have traveled all the way from the Eifel to warn you!"

"Aaach! Premonitions! Superstitions! Let us be off!"

Herman Joseph stepped quickly in front of the bishop's horse, causing it to rear. Then he looked at Engelbert and from the depths of his soul pleaded once more, "Death lies in wait for you! My lord, do not ride to Schwelm!"

"I thank you, venerable Father, for your warning, but my resolution is firm. I must ride on and entrust my life to the hand of God. Onward!"

Hoofbeats thundered around the old canon as he watched the riders gallop away. Then he slowly walked through the streets of Cologne, the city which had been so familiar to him in his childhood years. He tried to recall those happy days, but his heart was now heavy with sorrow.

He returned to the cemetery of Sankt Mergen and prayed over the graves of his parents and Sister Iburga. Then he prayed before the statue of the little Madonna, to whom he had once given an apple. However, his heart remained uncomforted. On the trip home, he did not speak one word to his companion, Brother Bruno.

\* \* \*

Evening approached as the archbishop and his entourage rode through a deep gorge. Engelbert had been withdrawn during most of the journey. He could not forget the face of the priest from the Eifel and his warning. He had been tempted to heed his warning and return, but he decided to continue.

Suddenly, a shrill whistle pierced the sound of the rumbling hoofbeats. A horde of armed men rushed from the nearby woods and attacked the archbishop's men. His retinue was too stunned to react. Only Count Conrad of Dortmund defended Engelbert. He was struck to the ground and the archbishop himself was overpowered by nearly a dozen men. Pitchforks, spears, and axes fell upon him. When they were sure he was dead, these allies of Count Frederick returned to Isenburg.

A farmer's manure cart carried the corpse of the archbishop to Schwelm. Four days later his body was returned to Cologne where Engelbert was laid to rest in the cathedral. The bishop's murderers did not escape punishment, and Frederick himself was also executed. But Engelbert's archdiocese, his principality, and all the empire had lost a good and noble prince.

* * *

Severe eye trouble had afflicted Herman Joseph ever since the night of the archbishop's murder. A fiery sign in the sky above Cologne had appeared to him. When he saw it, he knew his premonition about Engelbert had been correct. Herman Joseph traveled once again to Cologne where he prayed over the archbishop's grave, and at once recovered from his affliction.

"He is a saint!" said the canon when he returned to the Eifel. "We don't need to pray for him. He prays for us. Cologne has lost a good bishop, but the city has gained a new patron in heaven!"

# Chapter Twenty Two
# Perfect Joy and the Two Apples

It's true! Father Herman Joseph performs miracles!" exclaimed Sister Mechtild, the kitchen Sister of Hoven. "He arrived here during a very hot spell last summer. Father asked me for a drink of water, and I handed him an empty pitcher. I wanted to see if he would scold me. There was not a drop of water in that pitcher, but Father held it to his mouth and drank! Then he looked at me as only Father Herman Joseph can and thanked me for the refreshment. I could not say a word in response."

"And I have heard stories from Steinfeld," continued Prioress Ruxtell. "The Mother of God replaced two of his teeth and healed his broken arm! He must be a very great saint."

"I'm not sure that everything you hear is true," said Abbess Gertrude. "But I know that mothers come to him from all over the Eifel asking him to bless their children. Yes, he is a very good and pious man."

"He is a holy man," Sister Elizabeth quietly added. "Today our Blessed Lady appeared to me and said, 'Father Herman Joseph is my chaplain. Receive him with proper respect.'"

"You are lucky, Sister," sighed Sister Euphemia. "The Mother of God always appears to you, but to me it's always the devil. He never leaves me alone."

"Have faith, Euphemia," the abbess consoled her. "He did not spare even the Lord."

"Yes, we must receive Father Herman Joseph with proper respect by all means," said Sister Hildegunde, the sacristan. "The altar boys should swing the censers before him as we do for the bishop. Afterall, he's the *chaplain* of the Mother of God!"

"I am very much ashamed," confessed Sister Elizabeth, "that I used to scold him in my heart for saying the Mass so slowly."

"I don't know what to cook for him," interrupted Sister Mechtild. "But why do I worry? Father doesn't even notice what he swallows. I asked him once what he thought of the salmon I had prepared for him. He said he didn't even realize he'd been eating salmon! I guess even the greatest saints have their little faults. Whoever doesn't notice what he's eating is missing a little shine on his halo."

* * *

139

Meanwhile, Herman Joseph was sitting in the house of Father Joseph, a very learned canon who lived in the Eifel village of Loewenich. Herman Joseph loved to stop there on his journeys to Hoven. At eighty-two years of age, he still walked the long distance, but he allowed himself the luxury of spending the night at Father Joseph's rectory. Heavy snowfall had made this trip especially difficult for the old canon, and he was comforted to see that Father Joseph had lit a big fire in anticipation of his arrival.

"Do you want another glass of hot milk, Father?" Joseph asked.

"No thank you, Joseph. But please tell me more of the holy *poverello* of Assisi. You met this man named Francis? Please tell me about him!"

"Father, my words are too poor to explain the beauty of this man. The world was paradise wherever he set his foot. He was the joyful song played by the Heavenly Musician. He loved all living things as his brothers and sisters, and between him and them there was a miraculous mutual understanding."

"Continue, Father Joseph. You are speaking most eloquently."

"Francis was a most cheerful beggar. He said that the person who has nothing is rich, for each day he must share in the love and mercy of both God and man. He said that poverty is holy."

"Poverty is holy!" smiled Herman Joseph. The words recalled the pretzels of Saint Joseph and Margaret, the friend of his childhood days, who had long ago found her final resting place in the cloister cemetery. "Oh, Joseph, if only I could begin again! I'd like to go begging with the *Poverello*."

"He was the ever-joyful brother. He spoke of nothing else so much as joy – perfect joy."

"Perfect joy! Yet he had to suffer much, I am sure."

"More than any other. The Lord afflicted him heavily with various ailments and poor health. But that is the strange thing. He said that suffering is perfect joy, for it makes us like Christ. Suffering is the hard outer shell, but the kernel inside is salvation!"

The old priest closed his eyes and meditated on what he had just heard. He, too, had suffered much, and how often he had lost all courage. And now he heard the paradoxical expression of "joyful suffering." Herman Joseph yearned to start all over again.

"I don't think you are much different from the *Poverello*," Father Joseph said. "No, you are very much like him, indeed."

* * *

When he was leaving the next morning, Herman Joseph requested two red apples from his host.

"Won't they be too hard for you?" laughed Joseph. "You have already lost several teeth, although the nuns at Hoven say the Mother of God is your dentist."

"The nuns at Hoven have hearts like children," the old priest remarked with a smile. "And for that, one must love them. But the apples are not for me, Joseph. I need them for my exorcisms. You see, I drive out the devil with them."

Once again, the old Premonstratensian had left Father Joseph speechless.

* * *

Sister Elizabeth sat for much of the morning in the belltower waiting for the priest from Steinfeld to arrive. When she saw him coming, she began to ring the bells. As she did so, many bats flew out of the tower. The sight of this made Herman Joseph smile as he recalled another memory from his youth. Then he was astounded to see the reception the nuns had prepared for him: the sisters were waiting with burning censers, singing the *Benedictus*:

> *Blessed is He Who comes in the name of the Lord.*
> *Hosanna in the highest!*

"You are mistaken, venerable Sisters! Henry of Molenark is the new bishop, not me." Then he respectfully greeted the abbess and the other nuns. Sister Euphemia was still quite pale because the devil had been troubling her again. Herman Joseph presented her with two beautiful, red apples.

"Here, Euphemia, these work well against the devil. Surely we must fight the enemy with his own weapons!" the priest said with a laugh.

"You should have Sister Euphemia do more farming," Herman Joseph suggested to Abbess Gertrude. "More fresh air and fresh food will help against evil thoughts."

"But she embroiders such beautiful vestments!" the abbess said in response.

"Yes, and then she has time to brood. No, no, Lady Abbess, farming is the right thing for her."

That evening Herman Joseph spoke about perfect joy. All the Sisters' hearts were brightened, even Sister Euphemia's. The apples and Saint Francis had done her much good.

* * *

The next morning was bitter cold, and the cloister chapel felt even colder than outdoors. The celebrant of the Mass was the only one who did not seem to feel the weather. He said the prayers more slowly than ever, and he stopped altogether after the Consecration. He asked the Incarnate God Whom he now held before him, "Lord, give them perfect joy!"

The Sisters were nearly frozen in the pews. One could have prayed a rosary more quickly than Father Herman said the *Memento*. Mechtild yearned for her warm kitchen stove, even though she was better equipped against the cold than the others. One of the altar boys finally took pity on the nuns and tugged hard at the priest's vestments.

Some of the Sisters grumbled afterwards, but the hot morning soup helped ease their suffering. Sister Euphemia, however, had never seemed so happy as on this bitterly cold morning. The sorrow, which had afflicted her for so long, left her completely.

## Chapter Twenty Three
# The Canticle of Canticles

**S**oon after Mass Herman Joseph began to shake violently and his body grew burning hot. The Cistercian nuns wrapped him in blankets and propped him up on pillows, ignoring the old priest's protests. Sister Mechtild brought a large pot of hot beer, which she gently made him drink.

Despite the nuns' efforts, Herman Joseph grew feverish to the point of delirium. Sister Hildegunde, who knew something about sicknesses, shook her head doubtfully. "There is nothing more we can do. The illness has seized his lungs. If only he were younger. It will take a miracle to make him well again."

"Then we must pray!" urged Sister Euphemia. "He taught us how to pray the Rosary; now we must pray it for him."

The fever continued, however, and in his delirious state, Herman Joseph again saw the spinning lights of the stars, which he had beheld on that winter night.

"Look! There it is – the Cross in the flames! Lord, extend Your arms far and wide! Take me with You on the Cross! They have pierced Your Heart! All the flames have enveloped Your Heart!"

Then the sick canon recoiled in his bed as if his own heart had been pierced with a flaming lance.

Sister Euphemia ceaselessly fingered her Rosary beads, praying for the canon's miraculous recovery. No one noticed the freezing cold of the chapel any more. Indeed, the entire community would have gladly endured an even longer Mass if only the good Father were to stand at their altar once again.

Sister Mechtild continued to bring hot stones and hot beer, and the combination of loving care and fervent prayer soon produced the miraculous cure they had all hoped for. The Sisters joyfully sang the *Te Deum* when they heard that Father Herman's fever had finally broken.

Herman Joseph felt as if God had shown him the world's innermost secrets during the worst of his fever. "The Heart is the center of the world!" he whispered softly to Sister Euphemia, "the Heart of Golgotha."

"You are too weak to write!" the Sister protested when Herman Joseph sat up in bed and asked for parchment, ink, and a quill.

"I must write down the song which God has given me!" Then the canon composed the first hymn ever written in honor of the Sacred Heart of Jesus:

*Hail, Heart of Jesus, King Supreme!*
*All hail, my happy song's great theme!*
*I long Thy beauty to possess,*
*Yet wonder that Thy holiness*
*Should bide my sinful breath.*

*How great the love that conquered Thee,*
*And yet how deep the pain must be,*
*That God should habit as a slave,*
*And be as one of us, to save*
*Mankind from endless death.*

*Then Death, enhungered, could not bear*
*The Heart of God Himself to spare,*
*But gnawed a pathway to the cell*
*Wherein the Life of life doth dwell,*
*With bitter, envious tooth.*

*Oh Heart of God, broken for me*
*Upon the Cross of Calvary,*
*Be this my prayer, my sole desire:*
*That my poor heart, at length afire,*
*May love in deed and truth.*

*Pierce, dearest Love, with fiery dart,*
*The inmost fibers of my heart!*
*Oh let me feel the quivering wound*
*Of answering love each soul hath found*
*That once embraceth Thee.*

*The witful lance that pierced Thy side*
*Hath opened fountains that abide*
*To wash my soul of every sin,*

*To cleanse without, to heal within,*
*To make me whole and free.*

Spiritual flames enkindled the poet's own heart, and once again Herman Joseph felt the pierce of the red-hot lance, just as he had during his fever; just as he had when he climbed over the choir gate as a young boy to approach the Mother of God.

*Open like a rose, O Heart most fair!*
*And let me breathe thy fragrance rare!*
*Bind mine to Thee, and let it prove*
*The deepest pangs and joys of love –*
*Who loves can suffer naught.*

*Although He knows the rugged way,*
*His flying feet He cannot stay;*
*To love He placeth bound nor mete;*
*A thousand deaths to Him are sweet*
*Whom love at last hath caught.*

*Live, live, O Love, in ecstasy;*
*'Live, live, O Love,' alone I cry.*
*Come close and closer to my heart;*
*Embrace me, never to depart;*
*Be mine forevermore!*

*In Thy love alone let me live,*
*To slumber ne'er a moment give!*
*Whether I pray, or sing, or weep,*
*Let me perpetual vigil keep*
*To love Thee and adore!*

*O Heart of Jesus, blood-red Rose,*
*Open wide thy petals and disclose*
*The outer grace, the inner bloom,*
*And let me breathe the rich perfume*
*That steals my sense away!*

The priest-poet somehow found the strength to scribble verse after verse onto the parchment. Every now and then he sank back onto his pillow, totally exhausted. Sister Euphemia continued to pray her Rosary. She didn't dare take the quill from Herman Joseph's hand. Then he struggled to sit up again. Sister prayed, struck with a sense of awe and wonder, when she saw the ethereal light in the priest's eyes as he finished his song.

*Great Lover, draw my heart to Thee!*
*Spurn not my sinful misery,*
*But let me find my sweetest rest*
*Within the chamber of Thy breast,*
*There to recline for aye!*

*Thither I fly, there I shall stay,*
*To be Thy comrade on the way;*
*There shall I learn to know Thy Will.*
*Of that blest Fount to drink my fill*
*And know Thee as Thou art.*

*Even on earth my joy shall be*
*Wholly to give myself to Thee;*
*Forbid me not to enter in –*
*Thou cam'st on earth my love to win,*
*Supremely loving Heart!*

✳ ✳ ✳

Herman Joseph returned to Steinfeld in the spring. The cloister had wanted to send a wagon for him, but he refused. He wished to return on foot so he could enjoy nature's beauty emerging from the winter snows. "Life sings the *Te Deum* during spring!" remarked the old canon to his young escort, Father Wilfrid.

"Yes, spring," answered Wilfrid, "the time when life bursts open, and storms pass through the land."

Herman Joseph saw the young man's earnest expression and knew well that Wilfrid was thinking about the time when the storm of youth had passed through the spring of his own life. He had not lost the vigor and conviction which had impelled him to raise the banner of Christ for the Children's Crusade.

"I wish I could travel to the East, to Bohemia, to Silesia, to Hungary or to Prussia," Wilfrid sighed. "That's where the great, holy storm is. In those places a new spring is emerging. Knights

146

have recently carried Christ's banner into the pagan East. They're building a human wall against unbelievers and the Muslims. More knights are now storming through Prussia to the East. They must struggle against the spears of the enemy as well as against the fangs of wolves, against wild beasts and bears. German settlers have departed from Westphalia, Flanders, and Frisia. They know the difficult struggles and dangers that await them, but they continue to set out for this new land. Magnificent castles have been built in Kulm, Thorn, Marienwerder, and Christburg, and the new land has been consecrated to Our Blessed Lady: *Terra Mariana*."

"The Land of Mary!" Herman Joseph repeated respectfully. Then he heard the ringing of the *Angelus* bells from the nearby churches of the Eifel. "Our land is also the 'Land of Mary'!"


After they prayed the *Angelus*, Wilfrid continued petulantly, "I want to go east! What good can I do at Steinfeld? I'm supposed to help old Father Anthony with his illuminations, but tomorrow many of our brothers are traveling to our cloisters in Bohemia. I don't understand why the abbot won't let me go along with them."

"Obedience stands above all, Wilfrid! Prayer and sacrifice build a wall which no one can breach."

They walked in silence the rest of the way. Finally, the towers of Steinfeld could be seen rising in the distance. The old priest's jubilation at seeing his familiar home was mixed with the young man's pain.

A cheer erupted from the confreres and students when they saw Herman Joseph approach. When the old canon returned to his cell, he discovered that it was once again filled with flowers. "That's a greeting from your boys!" Father Anthony told him. "I have never seen the fellows pray so hard as when you were sick." Tears welled up in both men's eyes.


Later, Herman Joseph visited Father Anthony in the *scriptorium*. He was the only one of Herman's boyhood friends who was still alive. Albert, Arnulf, and Rudolph had all passed away long ago, and, just one year earlier, news had come from Bohemia that Father Conrad died from a severe fever.

"I'm working on the *Canticle of Canticles*," Anthony answered his old friend when asked about his current project. "This should be my final work. See, my hand is getting shaky. But I want to do this illumination before I finally lay down my quill!"

"Yes, Anthony, the *Canticle* is the proper finale!" As Herman Joseph read the magnificent verses of the first chapter, his soul heard a ringing which was not from this world.

The next morning, Herman Joseph burst into his old friend's cell. "Anthony! I want to write a commentary on the *Canticle of Canticles*. I want to open men's ears to the sound of heaven!"

His confrere smiled at him and said, "The great Origen has written an explanation of the *Canticle of Canticles*, as well as Theodore of Cyrus, Gregory of Nyssa, and even Abbot Bernard of Clairvaux. But theirs are not enough. You, Herman, will provide the true explanation!"

"Oh, you must not mock me," Herman Joseph said. "Last night the Mother of God appeared to me in a dream. She carried a large, bright urn, and said, 'This is the *Canticle of Canticles*: take it and draw it out.' When I told her the container seemed empty, she smiled and said, 'It is not quite empty yet. Look closely!' Then I saw a little bit of oil at the bottom of the urn. 'You are to scoop that out!' Mary said. And then she vanished.

"So now you see, Anthony, why I will take up the quill to write a commentary on the *Canticle of Canticles*. I will blend the melodies from the holiest of hearts: the Sacred Heart of Jesus and the Immaculate Heart of Mary. I only ask that God allow me to live long enough to finish it."

## Chapter Twenty Four
# The Mongol Flood

**W**hen Father Anthony finally completed his illumination of the *Canticle of Canticles*, even Wilfrid was overwhelmed by the beauty of the splendid letters the old master had painted. The young canon now thanked God for sending him to work in Father Anthony's cell. The elderly artist wrote a short epilogue: "Christ, I have written this for you and for the honor of Our Blessed Lady. Now I am tired. Dear reader, pray for the illuminator of this book." With that, he laid down his brush and died.

The artist's old friend continued working on his own *Canticle of Canticles*. Herman Joseph knew that he would not join Anthony in heaven until he had completed his commentary. However, he sometimes spent weeks contemplating just one verse. And very often he felt that his words were too dull a reflection of the verse's radiant beauty which he carried in his heart. Then he would tear up what he had just written and return to his holy ruminations inspired by the *Canticle*. The outside world was torn with conflict, but the cell of the silent canon was filled with a heavenly peace.

The Guelfs and the Ghibellines were at odds over papal authority. Though Pope Gregory IX was nearly one hundred years old, he fought with vengeance against Frederick II, the Hohenstaufen, who also had to contend with his own rebellious son Henry. Legions of knights and farmers continued to fortify the 'Land of Mary.' The world was no less clamorous than before.

Herman Joseph was now ninety years old, and he longed for eternity. His body was bent, but his mind was still sharp, and he knew that he would not rest until he had completed the commentary.

"The urn which Mary showed me is still not empty. Like the widow of Zarephath's jug, the oil has no end. I simply cannot empty it, Wilfrid."

"How far are you, Father Herman Joseph?"

"I'm on the last chapter! Listen:"

*Set me like a signet ring on your heart,*
*Like a seal on your arm!*
*For strong as death is love!*

*Like an abyss, its demand is immense,*
*Its torches are a flaming, glowing fire!*
*No amount of water is able to quench love,*
*And all rivers do not inundate it.*

After reading it, he said with a trembling voice, "Brother, I will never exhaust this."

"Take your time, Father. We would like to have you with us for a few more years."

"Now I know what eternity is. For many years I have tried, but I can find no end to the richness of this song. When the soul of man can empty God in all His richness, that is heaven."

Word spread around the cloister that the venerable priest would die after he had completed his work. Thus, the old canon was often approached by young students who urged him to take his time with his commentary on the *Canticle*.

"Yes, the Song of Solomon needs much time," he would respond with a smile. "I will have all eternity to sing it!"

**✻ ✻ ✻**

The feast of the Holy Innocents in the year 1240 brought a special surprise. As usual, the young Latin student received the cantor's staff while the choir sang the *Magnificat*:

*He has cast down the mighty from their thrones*
*And has exalted the lowly.*

And then as customary, one of the boys sat on the throne in the chapter hall, holding the abbot's silver staff. One of his proclamations rang out:

"I forbid Father Herman Joseph from finishing his commentary on the *Canticle of Canticles*. We all need him too much. We students took our new positions at the point when the *Magnificat* praises the humble. But there is no one in Steinfeld who is as humble as Father Herman Joseph. Therefore, I order him to take over as abbot for the day!"

The chapter hall resounded with applause, and the abbot whispered to the prior, "The boy is right. No one has a more gentle heart than Father Herman Joseph."

"Yes," agreed the prior. "He has preserved his childlike nature despite his ninety years. His whole being is radiant with grace. He has told me much about his childhood, and it's so beautiful that I have recorded it on paper without our dear confrere's knowledge. People will still be speaking about him when we are long gone and forgotten!"

The students led the old priest to the throne despite his mild resistance. Finally he accepted the silver staff and, raising his hand for silence, he spoke:

"My predecessor has forbidden me to finish my commentary on the *Canticle of Canticles*. Yes, I know well that when it is finished I will die. Therefore, as abbot of Steinfeld, I order Father Herman Joseph to complete his work by the beginning of Holy Week. When the Easter bells ring out, his confreres will be singing his *Requiem*."

✳ ✳ ✳

A few days later, Abbot Macarius assembled the community in the chapter hall. "We have received some bad news from our cloisters in Bohemia and Silesia," he announced in a grave tone. "Mongols are riding toward the West. The 'Mongol flood' of Genghis Khan has punished the Russian principalities and is moving through Galicia and Poland. It threatens the very borders of our empire. Wherever they ride on their small, swift horses, death and destruction reign. The emperor is away in Italy, but if the 'Mongol flood' is not halted at the German border, the empire, and even Christendom, will perish.

"Our brothers in the East need help! Priest, knight, and farmer: all three are needed to strengthen the wall against the East. A new wave of Frisian and Westphalian settlers wish to travel to Bohemia. Several of us must go along. It may very well be a journey to death, so I will not order anyone to go. I only ask for volunteers."

Many of the young canons sprang to their feet, and even some of the older ones approached the abbot. Father Wilfrid led the group. The abbot's eyes were sparkling with pride for the sons of Norbert as he called out six names. Wilfrid wanted to cry out for joy as he heard his name, but he maintained a stoic expression that revealed only his fierce determination.

"I once left Steinfeld without your blessing, but I will not do it again," Wilfrid declared as he bade farewell to Herman Joseph.

"You have truly been like a father to me, so bless me as a father blesses his child – a child he will never see again."

Herman Joseph laid his hands upon the head of his young confrere. "May God bless you, Wilfrid!" After a long pause he added, "You ride to death. My path is the same, though I travel on foot. I bless you as a father blesses his son. Yet I know that we will see each other again!" He finally, and feebly, pulled the young man from his knees and squeezed his hands without saying another word.

The horses were mounted and, after they galloped out of the cloister courtyard, the sound of their pounding hooves echoed for a long time. Herman Joseph waited until he could hear it no more. Then he walked to the church and once again asked God for the chalice of suffering.

\* \* \*

Kneeling almost continuously before the tabernacle, the ninety-one-year-old priest offered up his life to God for those on their death march. A most intense pain afflicted his body, and an overwhelming anguish gripped his soul. Yet Herman Joseph was not oppressed by this suffering as he once had been. He often saw the face of the poor man of Assisi, who seemed to say, "Have courage! In suffering there is hidden perfect joy."

Lent arrived, and the bells rang out their heavy summons to reflection and penance. The need for sacrifice and atonement grew even stronger, as terrible reports of the 'Mongol flood' arrived from the East. Herman Joseph continued working on his commentary while maintaining his intensified vigil of prayer.

One day a messenger arrived from the Cistercian nuns at Hoven requesting a priest to help with their Holy Week services. They asked specifically for Father Herman Joseph. At first the abbot refused because the journey was too difficult for one so old. However, the elderly canon pleaded with such childlike earnestness that Abbot Macarius eventually gave in.

Herman Joseph finally finished his commentary on the *Canticle of Canticles* on Passion Sunday. He laid down his quill, exhausted almost to the point of death. When his confreres congratulated him, he said, "It is nothing. Only a faint echo of all the glorious music of God which, for the past nine years, has filled my cell and my soul." Then he prepared for his journey to Hoven.

One day, before leaving Steinfeld for the last time on Wednesday of Passion Week, Herman Joseph knelt in prayer longer than usual before the tabernacle. He reflected on all the joy and comfort he had experienced there for nearly eighty years.

When the time came for his departure, he silently left his cell, leaving behind the other canons, the students, and the graves of his beloved confreres. As he was leaving the cloister grounds, he looked up at the massive abbey tower and told his student escort, "Almost eighty years ago I drove the bats out of that tower with the help of Saint Augustine. Yes, this has been my home, my Bethany. But now we go up to Jerusalem."

* * *

The canons from Steinfeld and settlers from the Eifel rode into Breslau, which looked more like an army camp than the capital of Silesia. A large troop of Teutonic knights entered the city at the same time as the Norbertines. The knights were clothed in long, loose mantles with a cross on each shoulder, and on their banners waved the black eagle of the German Empire.

Wilfrid galloped to the castle of Duke Henry, carrying a message from Abbot Macarius. The son of the saintly Duchess Hedwig read the note and exclaimed, "You want to go to Bohemia! It takes great courage, indeed, to ride to the East these days. The Mongols are now approaching Liegnitz. You must hurry, otherwise the routes to Bohemia will be blocked."

"We do not want to ride to Bohemia until the battle with the Mongols begins!"

"You want..."

"...to fight along with you, Duke Henry!" Wilfrid enthusiastically completed the Duke's sentence.

"Dear Father, there are countless numbers of Mongol horsemen. We are only a few. We will surely be sacrificed in battle!"

"Then we will die with you!"

Duke Henry firmly clasped the hands of the young canon and said, "I thank you, and I welcome you! If our weapons cannot stop the enemy, then God will surely see our courageous sacrifice. Perhaps, on account of it, He will spare our beloved empire!"

153

## Chapter Twenty Five
# A Gate Springs Open

**H**erman Joseph and his student escort made the customary rest stop in Loewenich at the home of Father Joseph. The two visitors stared at the crackling flames in the hearth, listening to the beautiful, mystical words recited by their host. He read from the last verses of Francis' song, *The Canticle of the Sun*:

> *Praised be You, O Lord,*
> *For our Sister Bodily Death,*
> *From whom no living man*
> *Can escape!*
>
> *Woe to those who die in mortal sin!*
> *But blessed be those who have discovered*
> *Your most holy will;*
> *For to them the second death*
> *Can do no harm!*
>
> *Praise and bless my Lord*
> *And give Him thanks, all creation,*
> *And serve Him*
> *With great humility!*

Father Herman Joseph spoke softly but with great fervor: "This is the joy which welcomes death itself. This is perfect joy! It is beautiful to die this way."

"Yes, my brother. Francis himself died singing, although his body was tortured with pain. The stigmata of the Lord's wounds were impressed onto his hands, feet, and side."

"So he bore the five holy wounds?!"

"Yes, Father. He received the Lord's greatest blessing: to be taken onto the Cross with Him!"

Herman Joseph then recalled the distant days of his childhood when he suffered from the severe fever after the great fire in Cologne. He, too, had cried out to the Lord, "Take me onto Your Cross! I want to hold my arms over the flames and extinguish the fire." The sacred flame in his soul had burned ever more brightly since that day long ago.

* * *

Palm Sunday at Hoven was made even more special by the arrival of Herman Joseph and his young escort. Once again, the entire cloister sang his welcome with joyful reverence, and the altar boys swung their censers. "This is my Palm Sunday," he thought. "So my hill of Calvary cannot be far away."

"My dear Sister Euphemia! How are you? Do you still need a few apples?" Herman Joseph asked with a bit of tender humor.

"There is no need, Father." Blushing, she vigorously shook her head.

Herman Joseph suddenly stopped as they walked through the cloister hall. Then he traced a rectangle on the stone floor with his walking stick, saying: "Here you will bury my body."

Fear came over the nuns' faces. Herman Joseph smiled, though, and said, "Dear Sisters, do not be afraid. The grave is a good bed, and death is our brother who takes us home to our Father."

With extreme difficulty, the old priest performed the sacred services of the first days of Holy Week. On Tuesday he was reading Saint Mark's Passion when a burning fever inflamed his body. He finished celebrating the Holy Sacrifice of the Mass, but collapsed at the altar steps afterward, his body bathed in sweat.

The Sisters rushed him to bed, terrified by the knowledge that a dying man was there before them. Some of those attending him blamed themselves for asking the beloved priest to journey so far. However, Herman Joseph recovered consciousness long enough to console them: "It is good this way, Sisters. At Steinfeld I felt at home to live. Here I feel at home to die." Then he made one request: "In your church stands a statue of the enthroned Madonna. Would you please bring it here? I surely need my Mother now."

After the Sisters had fulfilled his wish, he smiled and said, "Now I can die under the eyes of my Mother!" A beam of joy flashed from his old eyes. Then he fell once again into a feverish delirium. He dreamed of burning cities, charging knights, and the 'Mongol flood.'

* * *

The flood of Mongols overwhelmed the West. Poland fell without much resistance, and flames consumed Cracow. The villages surrounding the capital of Hungary also burned like torches. The

155

archbishop's army was cut to pieces and the city was stormed. Its inhabitants were murdered, and Mongol boys were rewarded for cracking the skulls of young Magyars.

The invaders from the East continued their westward campaign of burning and carnage towards Moravia and Silesia. Churches in the eastern part of Germany were filled with people who prayed with fervent entreaty: "Lord, save us from the fury of the Tartars!"

\* \* \*

Father Joseph arrived from Loewenich on Good Friday and heard Herman Joseph's last confession.

"Oh, dear brother!" moaned Herman Joseph, "what has my life been? Our Lady asked me to bear the Savior throughout the world. And what have I done? I have sought nothing but rest and peace in my quiet cell. I have sought after myself when I should have been attending to the needs of my poor, lost brothers."

"You have sought God in stillness," Father Joseph responded, "and you have done much good for your brothers. God lays different burdens on different men. One he sends to preach and to convert, another to do battle with word and sword. God has chosen you for the work of penance, for a life of prayer and stillness. God only knows how many blessings your sacrifices have brought into this world!"

The dying man only moaned again: "No, no, brother! My life was nothing! If only I could start over again! That would be beautiful!"

"You have earned your peace, Herman Joseph! Your life has been rich in grace and has yielded much fruit. You carry sheaves to the heavenly harvest."

But Herman Joseph did not hear him. He had sunk again into unconsciousness. In this state he was tormented by ominous visions of his threatened homeland.

\* \* \*

"I can wait no longer!" stormed Duke Henry of Silesia as he paced heavily before his senior general. "I cannot wait for the King of Bohemia to arrive. The Tartars have invaded my land. They are burning my villages, destroying our lands, murdering my people, and you say I should wait?!"

"My lord!" answered the knight, "It is not cowardice which causes me to tell you to wait. We are so few. The enemy waiting for us at Liegnitz is five times our size!"

"Then God must be on our side! He will not allow our sacrifices to count for nothing."

A noble lady dressed in widow's garb entered the room. The old knight bowed deeply before her and said, "Noble Duchess, please admonish your son to be prudent. We must wait for the Bohemian forces!"

Duchess Hedwig responded, "Mothers have come carrying their children. They cry to me and beg for help. I have promised them help." Turning to her son, she urged, "Do your duty, Duke of Silesia. God will be with you!"

Henry the Pious warmly held Lady Hedwig's hands: "I thank you, Mother. You have vanquished any doubts I had. Lord Knight!" he cried to his general, "Tomorrow is the day ordained by God. Whoever will join me in battle must first attend Mass and receive the Body of Christ. It will be our *Viaticum*. And, after Mass, we shall ride!"

"With reluctance I advised you to follow discretion, my lord," the general explained. "But now I am happy that you did not heed my counsel. God is with the brave of heart, my prince!"

"I am no longer your prince, good knight. Our prince is Saint Michael! His standard shall fly before us... and it may cover our corpses as well. With Saint Michael, for God and the Empire!"

"With Saint Michael, for God and the Empire!"

\* \* \*

The bells of Easter rang out over Hoven, but there was a note of sorrow in their pealing. Hearts were grieving for the dying priest and fearful over the empire's threat from the East.

"I see them riding!" stammered the feverish canon, gripping convulsively the hand of Father Joseph. "They're wearing white mantles with black crosses on them. I see the flash of their armor. The pages are wearing colorful frocks. Look, Joseph! There are flags flying, with Saint Michael holding a flaming sword. And one is riding in the Norbertine habit. He's holding the banner of Saint Michael with both hands! It's *Wilfrid!*" Then he sank back into unconsciousness.

Thirty thousand German nobles, knights, farmers, and miners rode off to battle on the morning of April 9, 1241. Wilfrid rode with the Frisian and Westphalian settlers carrying the standard of Saint Michael. They knew death was imminent, but that did not deter them. They could see the distant smoke from burning villages. With the bells of Eastertide ringing in the background, a battle song swelled up from the ranks of the soldiers:

> *O holy hero with invisible might,*
> *Lead our armies as we go to fight,*
> *Saint Michael, our Prince!*

* * *

During the first days of the Easter octave, Herman Joseph received the Holy Eucharist with clear senses. His anxiety had vanished, and a deep joy radiated from his eyes.

"This Easter celebration has always been very dear to me," he told Father Joseph who had brought him Holy Communion. "Beyond this 'day' lies the shimmer of eternal light! But on this day, many white garments will be stained red. Brother Death is wielding his sickle. In heaven there are other garments awaiting – robes whiter than snow. Please give me my Rosary, Joseph. I want to weave a wreath of white roses for the Mother of God."

* * *

At that same hour, Mongol and German troops were fighting in Wahlstatt, a small village near Liegnitz. Though the Germans were badly outnumbered, they fought with courage summoned by faith, not desperation. The mighty Duke of Silesia wielded his sword against row after row of Tartars, filling the streets with blood. Mongol horsemen stormed the wall of German warriors, but in vain.

"With Saint Michael, for God and the Empire!" The holy war cry resounded through the chaos. Wilfrid, the standard bearer, was already bleeding from many wounds. He remained in his saddle, however, and held the banner high over all the death and destruction.

* * *

The evening darkness began to fill the room at the cloister of Hoven where the Sisters knelt by the bed of the dying canon who had been like a father to them. Herman Joseph's eyes had been closed for a long time, and the attending priest had to hold his ear over the dying man's mouth to discern the slightest breath.

Then Herman Joseph looked up at the priest with clear, open eyes.

"Father Joseph," he whispered, "please tell me once more the last part of Francis' *Canticle of the Sun.*" The priest gladly complied:

> *Praised be You, O Lord,*
> *For our Sister Bodily Death,*
> *From whom no living man*
> *Can escape!*

Then Herman Joseph weakly raised his hand and finished the verse:

> *But blessed be those who have discovered*
> *Your most Holy Will;*
> *For to them the second death*
> *Can do no harm!*

\* \* \*

The darkened streets around Liegnitz were deathly quiet, and the half moon dimly illuminated the blood-soaked earth. The German forces had sacrificed to the last man. Among the dead lay Father Wilfrid, his hands still clutching the shaft of the banner. The flag of Saint Michael covered his body.

A single torch cast its light upon the face of Duchess Hedwig. She sat in the midst of the fallen soldiers, holding her dead son in her lap. In her eyes, however, there were no tears.

The hoofbeats of the retreating Mongols sounded ever more distant. The terrible losses they suffered at Wahlstatt drove them back to the Russian plains. The wall of sacrificial victims had stopped the Mongol flood.

\* \* \*

Herman Joseph's eyes grew dim as he gazed upon the statue of Mary. "Help me across to you!" he pleaded. "The gate to the choir

159

is closed. Mother, give me your hand! Help me over to you! A lance is piercing my heart! Yes, that is good, Mother! Yes, give me your hand! Take me into your lap! For in you … dear Mother … there is *Life!*"

* * *

Herman Joseph's body was buried in the convent at Hoven. Later, the canons of Steinfeld carried him home to their cloister in the Eifel.

"We lay to its final rest a heart which lived in stillness despite these tumultuous times," the abbot said over the grave. "But in that stillness, he accomplished great things which can only be measured by God. Herman Joseph stood as the keeper of the gate – the gateway to a new and great era emerging before us. He stood on the threshold of a new and powerful century. It shall be ruled by Mary, the one for whom his whole heart was enflamed. Herman Joseph, the canon of Steinfeld, opened the way to the *Century of Our Lady.*"

* * *

At that same hour, the master builder, Gerhard von Rile, stood before Conrad von Hochstaden, the archbishop of Cologne. He unrolled his designs before the prince of the Church. The archbishop was speechless.

"You dare to build that?" he gasped.

"With God's help and yours, my gracious lord!"

"The Cathedral of Mary on the Rhine!" exclaimed the archbishop. "Good. Then we will build it to the honor of Cologne."

The master builder added, "And to the honor and glory of the Holy Mother of God!"

# Historical Afterword

The ancient life of St. Herman Joseph, as indicated by Hünermann in his novel, was written by the prior of Steinfeld shortly after the death of the saint. This primary source for the life of St. Herman Joseph was published for the first time in 1627 by John Chrysostom Van de Sterre, the Premonstratensian abbot of St. Michael's in Antwerp under the title *Lilium inter spinas: vita B. Joseph presbyteri et canonici Steinfeldensis Ordinis Praemonstratensis.* The same life was published by the Bollandists in *Acta Sanctorum Aprilis*, I, Antwerp 1675, pp. 687-714. Hünermann is faithful to the primary source throughout his novel while making ample use of the novelist's creative prerogative. Although much of the ancient life is omitted in the novel, the character and personality of St. Herman Joseph are effectively and faithfully portrayed in the work.

***Herman Joseph's family and childhood in Cologne:*** The names and personalities of Herman Joseph's parents and childhood friends are fictional. Herman Joseph did grow up in poverty in the city of Cologne. As the novel recounts, his family had fallen into such a state of poverty that he had no shoes in the deep of winter. He excelled in studies and preferred the spiritual pursuit of "true greatness and nobility" (Hünermann's expression) to the usual games of his comrades (he also had a life-long devotion to St. Ursula and the eleven-thousand virgins). The handing of the apple to the Virgin (witnessed by Sister Iburga in the novel) is an actual event in the childhood of Herman Joseph, later recounted to his confreres before his death. Although Sister Iburga is a fictional character, she personifies the kind of assistance Herman Joseph's impoverished family would have sought and received from the neighborhood monastery (there was indeed an abbey of noble nuns attached to Sankt Mergen).

The Church of Sankt Mergen, as it was called in the dialect of ancient Cologne, is the Church of St. Mary of the Capitol, where Herman Joseph was privileged from his earliest years to hold intimate conversation with the Virgin Mother and the Christ Child. While Herman's friend Margaret is fictional, his climbing over the gate, the pain in his heart, and his playing with the Christ Child are all ecounted in the ancient life. The vision of Christ Crucified in the flames during a fire in the neighborhood of Herman Joseph's home is also found in the ancient life.

Hünermann's emphasis on Herman Joseph's love for poverty is an authentic characteristic of his life, though the means he uses to develop the theme, such as the "pretzels of St. Joseph,"(actually depicted on the ancient doors of the Church of St. Mary) are his own creation. The ancient life of Herman Joseph does not indicate that he was called "Joseph" by any of his childhood friends, although this practice started soon after his arrival at the abbey of Steinfeld, where the confreres were deeply touched by his spiritual intimacy with the Virgin Mary. The frequent allusion to the "three crowns" and the Three Kings was characteristic of the city privileged to house their relics and which to this day bears the three crowns on its flag.

*Steinfeld and Mariëngaarde:* Hünermann's description of Steinfeld and its inhabitants faithfully represents the typical monastic life in the Premonstratensian Order at the time. The different abbots, including St. Frederick of Mariëngaarde, are all historical figures who were closely connected with the daily life of Herman Joseph. Specific incidences related in the novel, such as the cleaning of the stables on his arrival and the clearing of the bats from the tower, are Hünermann's way of developing actual elements of the character of Herman Joseph and the early Premonstratensians. Hünermann visited Steinfeld (as it exists today) and took the detail of the head of the cat carved on the ancient stone washbasin from his own observation of the monastery.

Although the names of Herman Joseph's confreres are fictional, Hünermann relies on the ancient life to recreate many of the novel's scenes which he then embellishes with names and details lacking in the original life.

*Parallel Historical characters and events:* Hünermann recreates a rich historical backdrop for the novel, interweaving the life of Herman Joseph with the events and personages of his day. St. Bernard of Clairvaux, St. Hildegard of Bingen, St. Francis of Assisi, and St. Dominic are just a few of the personalities mentioned by Hünermann that dominated the period and whom Herman Joseph would have known by their reputation. There is no historical basis